Raoul Whitfi
much of his
was a membe
to the United
films, but soo... ...service, seeing combat duty in France in 1918. After the war, Whitfield became a reporter for the Pittsburgh *Post*. In 1926 he published his first story in *Black Mask,* where he also published the series that later became his first novel, *Green Ice,* received with high acclaim: Dashiell Hammett praised it as "280 pages of naked action pounded into tough compactness by staccato, hammerlike writing." Whitfield followed *Green Ice* with two more mysteries, *Death in a Bowl* and *The* Virgin *Kills* (all available as Quill Mysterious Classics), as well as several books of aviation adventure fiction. An unhappy second marriage and poor health cut short his writing career.

Otto Penzler, series editor of Quill Mysterious Classics, owns The Mysterious Bookshop in New York City. He is the publisher of The Mysterious Press and *The Armchair Detective* magazine. Mr. Penzler co-authored, with Chris Steinbrunner, the *Encyclopedia of Mystery and Detection,* for which he received the Edgar Allan Poe Award from the Mystery Writers of America.

THE *VIRGIN* KILLS

THE VIRGIN KILLS

RAOUL WHITFIELD

A Quill Mysterious Classic

SERIES EDITOR:
OTTO PENZLER

Library of Congress Cataloging-in-Publication Data

Whitfield, Raoul.
The virgin kills.

(Quill mysterious classics)
Originally published: New York : A. Knopf, 1932.
I. Title. II. Series.
PS3545.H656V56 1986 813′.52 85-19266
ISBN 0-688-02869-1 (pbk.)

Printed in the United States of America

First Quill Edition

1 2 3 4 5 6 7 8 9 10

CONTENTS

•1•

VIRGINS AFT

Torry Jones stood near the rail, forward on the port side, holding a megaphone to his lips. He had a gal on each side of him; they acted as though they didn't mind it at all. The yacht looked sweet in the setting sun; all ruddy and trim—and very, very big. There was music somewhere aft; it died as the dirty launch wallowed, engine silent, close to the knife-edged prow. Torry called in a stern voice:

"Ahoy there! What smart craft is that?"

I looked at O'Rourke, who was scowling, his big head turned a little toward me. The scar stood out clearly across his right cheek; whenever I saw the scar, I saw Dingo Bandelli slashing with a knife, saw O'Rourke trying to batter it aside with bare fists. He spat into the Hudson water now, looked at the yacht with contempt in his fine eyes.

"*Virgin!*" I heard him mutter. "Damn woman ship! Lousy, pretty thing!"

I said: "Steady. Tell this cutthroat pal of yours to get in close with this tub and let us aboard. Don't talk too much. Vennell doesn't pay for talk."

O'Rourke showed even, white teeth in a smile. He was a strange character for a man who had been a gang leader's bodyguard, a waterfront scrapper, a killer. He was a strange character for a newspaper columnist to be escorting aboard Vennell's yacht. Guests we were to be, but I suspected that Mick O'Rourke was to be a highly paid guest.

He said to the man at the wheel of the wallowing launch:

"Lay her in close—and let us get aboard, Hunch. Get over to see Benny tomorrow. Say I went to Montreal on a deal. After that, don't talk any."

The one at the wheel grinned foolishly, nodded. He pointed a stubby finger toward the yacht's name, painted in gold letters against white.

"You be careful—you Mick!" he said, with a grin.

Torry called down, through the megaphone:

"Good God—it's Al! Is *that* all we've been waiting for?"

One of the crew dropped a ladder. A gal with blond hair and baby-blue eyes giggled down at us. Torry sang out mockingly:

"And when you get that craft ashore, put her in the ways, sir—and heave to with soap and paint!"

He looked at the man at the wheel. Hunch raised his flat-nosed face.

"Yeah?" he said huskily. "Did you say your name was Bastard, sir?"

Torry looked shocked. The girl on his left gave a little squeal of surprise and vanished from sight. O'Rourke said to Hunch:

"Hell—can't you read signs?"

He gestured toward the yacht's name. Hunch shrugged and chuckled hoarsely. Torry whistled.

"Some of the tab's staff, Al?" he called down to me.

O'Rourke leaned toward my feet, to get his big fingers on luggage. I said softly:

"If you're going to blow up, don't come aboard, Mick. It's that kind of a trip."

O'Rourke lifted weight easily. He flashed me a swift smile.

"Vacation," he muttered. "With me yellin'—for our side."

I nodded, smiling. Torry stared over the side and widened his eyes as the big fellow gripped the rope ladder. He said:

"My God, is *he* coming aboard?"

O'Rourke tilted his face and said in a tone that was so changed it was startling:

"It's the Proteus Episode of *Ulysses,* you see. Joyce has me puzzled, there, confused. The color symbols, perhaps."

Torry lowered the megaphone and stopped acting. His mouth hung open. I said to O'Rourke as he started up the ladder:

"But not *too* much reading, Mick. You must save your eyes for the Greek translation."

Torry said with awe in his voice: "Mother of God!"

Mick O'Rourke hauled his bulk up the rope ladder, part of my luggage in his left hand. Torry and the megaphone vanished from sight. Canned music drifted down to Hunch and me. A baby voice was singing *boop-boop-a-doop* and *hot-cha-cha* melody.

Hunch got a silly expression on his killer face. He winked at me. A very pallid girl with almond-shaped eyes looked down at us. She said very correctly:

"Oh, my dear!"

Hunch pursed his lips, and the girl's face vanished. Unpolite sound reached me as I gripped the rope ladder, started up. I said to Hunch:

"Naughty, naughty!"

He laughed hoarsely, and the ancient engine of the dirty launch started its putt-putt sound. I reached the break at the rail, got feet on the deck. Mick O'Rourke was standing with his back to me, seven feet tall and a yard wide. His legs were apart; he was surveying the group who surveyed him. I picked out Torry and said:

"Is Vennell aboard?"

Torry took his eyes away from O'Rourke and nodded his head. He came forward a little. I gestured toward Mick.

"This is O'Rourke," I said. "Mick, this is Torry Jones. You may have read about him in my sheet. He flew the Atlantic."

Mick extended a hand and they shook. Torry said grimly:

"And without a copy of *Ulysses,* Mr. O'Rourke."

O'Rourke looked superior. It was strange the way he could do that.

"Matter over mind," he said lightly. "I presume you had sandwiches?"

Torry looked at me and shook his head slowly.

"Tunney started it, I suppose," he said. "Are they friends?"

I looked amazed. "Friends?" I said. O'Rourke and I exchanged glances, looking mildly amused. Torry said grimly:

"Was that a social error?"

I shrugged. "Mr. O'Rourke has little sympathy for G. B. S.," I said. "Unlike Tunney, you see. He feels G. B.'s a *poseur.*"

Torry said: "Oh."

Mick nodded his big head. Standing with his legs spread apart and his big hands at his sides, swaying a little, he looked like a Bellows lithograph come to life. "Yeah, sure," he said.

A young female came forward, not too timidly, and flashed Torry a smile.

"Is he the new champ, Torry?" she asked.

Torry gestured toward me. I bowed to the dark-haired gal.

"I'm not positive," I said, "but it seems to me that Mr. Lenz is still considered supreme. But then, Mr. O'Rourke has played auction and contract in only a few of the better London clubs."

The gal stared stupidly at Torry. Mick slapped his left leg, making crackling sound.

"Hell, yes!" he said. "That's right."

Torry made a feeble gesture toward me. "Take her," he said. "The *Virgin's* yours."

Mick took a step forward, toward the dark-haired gal. I caught him by the arm.

"He's kidding," I explained. "And he means the yacht, anyway."

The big fellow looked disappointed. "Sure," he said huskily. "it *would* be like that."

Torry whistled softly. He said: "Do you go upstream with us, Mr. O'Rourke, to the Regatta?"

Mick nodded. "Why not?" he replied.

I smiled at Torry. "He's always wanted to see the crews race," I explained. "I think his mother would have wanted him to."

Mick O'Rourke threw back his big head and roared with laughter. It boomed around the immaculate ventilators and things.

"Jees yes!" he said. "If she hadn't drunk herself to death!"

I smiled at the staring eyes of the group beyond Torry.

"Just his little joke," I said. "Do you know where we're quartered, Torry?"

Torry Jones half closed his brown eyes. "Up forward, down below," he said. "Is he with you?"

I looked surprised. "Of course," I said. "Mick does things for me."

Torry looked at O'Rourke, whose big eyes were going from gal to gal.

"What sort of things do you do for Al, Mr. O'Rourke?" he asked in a peculiar voice.

Mick chuckled. "This and that," he said finally.

I nodded. "This and that, here and there," I agreed.

Torry said: "Just now and then?"

"Yes and no," I replied.

Mick O'Rourke slapped the same thigh again. He roared with laughter.

"My candle burns at both ends," he said hoarsely. "I gotta hunch it'll be out before morning."

Torry looked at me and said: "One thing nice—we'll anchor off the finish line, below the bridges. The State Insane Asylum will be fairly close."

There was muttering in the group just beyond Torry and the dark-haired gal. I said cheerfully to Mick:

"They think we're crazy."

O'Rourke nodded, grinning. "It's a complex," he said. "Ain't it?"

A white-coated steward came along the deck and smiled at me.

"Mr. Connors?" he said.

I nodded. "And Mr. O'Rourke," I replied, and gestured toward Mick.

The steward bowed. "Suite B is prepared," he stated. "Mr. Vennell sends his compliments and is glad you have arrived, sir. May I show you the way?"

Mick said: "I gotta wash up—I'm dirty as a—"

"Of course you are," I cut in with speed. "See you later, Torry."

Torry Jones stared blankly at me. Then he pulled himself out of it.

"At the stern—the rest of the gals are back there," he said.

I nodded and started to follow the steward. Mick O'Rourke said huskily:

"Virgins aft, eh?"

Torry groaned. The others murmured. We went along the scrubbed deck, past polished things that shone red. Mick's big feet made heavy sound. We reached Suite

B, and the steward showed us buzzers. Then he went away.

Mick sat on a bed, got a large handkerchief from the pocket of his striped suit, and wiped his forehead. He swore with great feeling.

"Did it go, Al?" he breathed thickly. "Did it go?"

I said: "It *will* go, but you've got to tone down a little. Vennell mixes his crowds. Some of the gals may be decent."

Mick grunted. "On Vennell's yacht?" he said, with much doubt.

I smiled. "Just the same, take it easy," I warned. "Let me tell 'em—my way. You remember what you used?"

The big fellow frowned. "That *Ulysses* crack—and the one about the candle burning at both ends," he said.

I nodded. "Don't make it too thick—scatter the stuff a little," I said. "Try the one about the Passion Play next."

Mick brightened up. "The girls oughta like *that* one," he said.

I stared at him, but he was serious enough. That cheered me. If he had *me* winging, it was fairly certain the others would fall for it.

The steward tapped on the door of the suite and stated that Mr. Vennell would be in his cabin for the next half-hour. I said:

"We'll be right along."

Mick O'Rourke swayed a little on the bed, reached into a hip pocket, and got loose a snub-nosed gun. It gleamed blue-black in the electric's subdued glow. He regarded it as though he'd never seen it before.

I said grimly: "Well, well! Where'd that thing come from?"

Mick made a clicking sound that reminded me of my Aunt Fannie.

"Can you beat it?" he said. "Some guy must have slipped it to me."

I nodded. "Is that the one you used on Beedy?" I asked.

Mick looked puzzled. "Maybe," he said. "Or was that other rod—"

I cut in. "Never mind. Let's go along and see Vennell. You don't have to be funny with him. He's worth five million."

Mick said: "And he's killed a guy."

I nodded. The yacht was vibrating—there was sound that might have come from an anchor haul. It died away, and we felt movement. Mick O'Rourke got off the bed, slipped the snub-nosed gun into his pocket again.

"It's moving," he announced.

I said: "A yacht is a she. *She's* moving."

Mick grinned. "Sure, I know that."

I led the way from the suite and spotted the steward down the corridor a short distance. Music drifted down from the deck. There was shrill laughter. Behind me the big feet of Mick thumped heavy shoes against linoleum.

"Hot-cha-cha!" he hissed tonelessly. "Papa's gotta new racket now!"

2

Eric Vennell looked at Mick O'Rourke with his gray eyes slitted. He had a browned face, contrasted by the white wasitcoat and tie. His lips were thin and straight-lined and his features good. Vennell was handsome in a hard, deliberate way. His dinner clothes fitted exceedingly well; he had a small hip line and good shoulders. After he had shaken hands with Mick, he relaxed in a fan-backed chair and gestured gracefully toward bottles, ice, and ingredients on a small table.

Mick said: "Thanks, but I'm on the wagon."

Vennell widened his eyes and looked at me. I fizzed a Scotch and soda into an important-looking drink.

"Mick never was much of a drinker," I said.

Vennell had a hard tone, even when he joked.

"It's terrible stuff," he said. "But this is sort of a farewell party, a final trip. The *Virgin* gets her keel scraped after the Regatta."

Mick and I sat in chairs facing the owner of the yacht. We smiled and said nothing. Vennell spoke to me:

"Carleton said he was sending you up to cover the race—in your breezy way. He said it wasn't so much a news story as a slangy, smart-aleck column he wanted from you. I suggested you do it from the *Virgin*."

I nodded. "Good of you," I said. "Much more comfortable than any other way I can think about."

Vennell rose, went over, and snapped a lock on the cabin door. It was growing dark—lights of Riverside Drive slipped beyond the windows of the cabin. The yacht was steaming slowly, with little motion. Vennell seated himself again. He said in a low tone:

"Then I called you—about a bodyguard."

Mick O'Rourke leaned forward and took a cigarette from the large humidor. I smiled at Vennell.

"Mick was with Andy Dormer for six months, when Diamond Crass was hating Dormer," I said. "I wasn't running a column then—just sort of covering Broadway. Getting information. I had some that Mick thought I shouldn't use. We argued about it, and I didn't use it. Then Dormer thought things were quieter than they were. He started going places alone or with a woman. They found him in the East River one morning, but he hadn't drowned."

Eric Vennell's eyes were expressionless. Mick lighted a cigarette noisily.

"Guys don't drown on bullets," he observed.

Vennell nodded. I smiled and said: "Now and then I run into Mick. I figured he might be your man."

The yacht owner reached almost lazily into a vest pocket and produced a bill. He flicked it to Mick.

"Five grand," he said quietly. "It may mean staying up late nights. But only for a few. We reach Poughkeepsie around midnight. The races are tomorrow. We'll lay over, maybe two days. That depends. Then we drop back here. And you're through."

Mick fingered the bill and said huskily: "It don't sound too tough."

Vennell shrugged. "It's one of those things," he said. "I'm paying for the bullet you *may* catch. This is the first time the *Virgin*'s been on Hudson River water in eight years. There were reasons for staying away—and for coming back. I'm not telling them."

Mick said: "You're paying me to stick close—and to shoot first if it looks bad."

Vennell nodded. "You're with me," he said.

I sipped my whiskey and soda. "Mick is big and tough, Eric," I said. "I had to figure a stall for him. He looks big and tough. So I've given him some lines to mix in with his own. Sort of as if he'd been around and had picked up stuff here and there."

Vennell looked puzzled. "What sort of stuff?" he asked.

I said: "Highbrow, in a way. It had a neat effect when he came aboard. I think we got it over."

Vennell said: "Well, how does that help?"

I sipped some more of my drink. "It alibis him," I replied. "I'm going to spread the word that he's my find. A big bruiser, a roughneck reaching for higher things. He's my find, and you wanted me along. So I brought him. I want him against the background, for a book I'm thinking about writing. You fall hard for him, laugh once in a while at his stuff—and it'll give him a reason for sticking close to you. You like him—and you're the big boss."

Vennell slitted his eyes and looked at Mick's huge form.

"All right," he said, "but it's like this—"

He shifted his body a little and his right hand slipped under his dinner jacket, toward the left shoulder. His voice had risen a little. The chair on which Mick was sitting creaked suddenly. Mick said in a grunt:

"Uh—"

His body battered the table between Vennell and me out of the way—his left-hand fingers ripped the yacht-owner's hand away from the half-exposed shoulder holster. His right hand jerked Vennell's gun loose, tossed it toward a pillowed window seat. For a second the hand vanished—then it held his own snub-nosed weapon. He backed away from Eric Vennell.

"Now—" he said slowly—"was that nice?"

Eric Vennell adjusted his dinner jacket, stood up. His eyes came away from the breakage on the floor, went to the snub-nosed gun in Mick's right hand. The gun was held low and close to the big fellow's right side. Mick was smiling.

I said: "Thank God I was holding *my* drink."

Vennell smiled with his thin lips making a straight line. His eyes were on Mick's.

"It suits me," he said grimly. "You've got eyes and you move fast for a big man. The five grand entitled me to know about that."

Mick O'Rourke chuckled. He went over to the pillows of the window seat and picked up Vennell's gun. There was a tapping at the door. Vennell took the gun from the big fellow and smiled at me.

"Open it—it's probably Griggs," he said.

I opened the door, and the steward looked past me toward the broken glass on the floor. Vennell smiled at him and said:

"Get at this mess, Griggs, will you? I didn't know the Hudson could get so rough."

The steward's face was expressionless. Both Vennell and Mick had their guns out of sight. Mick said suddenly:

"It's the Passion Play influence, clearly."

Vennell fingered his tie and moved toward a mirror hung between two windows. The siren of the yacht wailed twice and drew a piping reply from some small craft. Vennell said:

"We've a gay crowd aboard. Some picture people. Torry Jones, Don Rayne—he captained and stroked Columbia last year. Jones is the flier, you know. Carla Sard—she's between screen epics and on from Hollywood. Cy Dana—the sportswriter. Sonia Vreedon, the daughter of Ben Vreedon, the California criminal lawyer. And ten or fifteen others. Perhaps not that many. How many, Griggs—know?"

The steward said: "Fourteen, sir, besides the ones you named. I can't recall their names."

Vennell grunted. "I shouldn't think so," he said. "Don't believe I can. Don't believe I'd wish to."

I grinned. "Just a good bunch going up to see California sweep things clear," I said.

Vennell faced me, his eyes suddenly sharp. He said:

"Think so, Al?"

I nodded. "Cinch," I replied. "Odds are two, two and a half to one. Practically all sportswriters agree. The battle is for second place, between Washington and Columbia."

Vennell said: "You think that way, eh?"

I nodded. He shrugged. "Pour me one of mine, Griggs," he said. "And another for Mr. Connors. Mick—won't you have one?"

Mick O'Rourke smiled and shook his head. "Sometimes it gets my eyes," he said. "It finished my grandmother."

Vennell said: "That so? Too bad."

The big fellow chuckled. "Hell, no," he said. "She was a louse."

Griggs sucked in his breath sharply. Eric Vennell looked startled, then looked at me questioningly.

I said: "Personally, I thought she was quite a charming old lady."

Mick looked at me with amazement. I showed a thumb toward Griggs, who was pouring a drink, his facial muscles twitching. Mick O'Rourke said:

"Yeah—when she was sober."

Vennell laughed a little. "I imagine she lived to a good old age," he said.

Mick nodded. "She said she was ninety-eight—but she was an awful damn liar," he replied.

I took a fresh glass from Griggs' fingers. Vennell lifted his, and Griggs went from the cabin, closing the door quietly behind him. His footfalls died along the corridor. Vennell looked at me and said:

"Here's to the best crew, Al."

I nodded. "And the next best—the one that finishes back of California," I said.

Vennell drank. He did it decisively. Mick stood near the door, looking cramped even in the large cabin.

"Are them oars heavy—the ones they use?" he asked suddenly.

Vennell looked at me and chuckled. I said:

"Crew's a tough racket, Mick. It takes guts."

Mick O'Rourke smiled at me, narrowed his fine eyes on Eric Vennell's.

"I stick to my ten-shot rod," he said grimly. "It does the same thing."

Eric Vennell did something that might have been a shiver. He lighted a cigarette and said cheerfully:

"I believe the crowd is up above—aft."

Mick O'Rourke looked at me, then turned his eyes toward the yacht owner.

"Do I get a tipoff?" he said. "Anything to help?"

Vennell shook his head. "Nothing," he replied. "And don't crowd me—it isn't that bad."

I said: "Just be around, Mick."

Vennell nodded. "That's it," he agreed. "Just be around."

"Well—I can't swim," Mick stated. "So it won't be hard to be around."

I said: "We'll get right and go up."

Vennell smiled: "For cocktails," he said. "I think Carla Sard said she'd invented one for the trip. Called the 'Regatta.'"

He went out and toward a companionway. We went back to Suite B. After the door was closed, I said to Mick:

"Well—what do you think of Vennell?"

The big fellow frowned at his spread-fingered hands. Then he shrugged.

"He's tough—and he's a liar," he said in a hard voice.

I sighed. "But you're not quitting."

He swore at me. "Quittin'?" he breathed huskily. "I *like* 'em that way."

3

Carla Sard said gaily: "It's the 'Regatta'—to be taken with a clean stroke and no splashing. If you're in form you sit up at the finish. I got the idea while I was in the tub, at the Plaza—"

Torry Jones cut in: "As if that Plaza bunch ever bathe!"

Cy Dana, short and thickset, tapped his small mustache with stubby fingers and nudged me with an elbow.

"The kid's got the stuff," he said in his husky voice. "You'd better watch that palooka of yours."

I shook my head and leaned against the aft rail. Mick sat across the deck, taking up a lot of space and watching activities with a silly grin.

"He's seen all this before," I said. "Only not on a yacht. He was a bouncer at the Lido for a time."

The sportswriter stared at me. "Bouncer at where?" he muttered.

I said: "Sure—at the Lido. But he made a mistake one night."

Dana grunted. "And bounced Moss and Fontana for doing a hot dance, I suppose?" he said.

I shook my head. "You were close," I told him. "It was Irene Bordoni—he chucked her out for doing one of those French songs."

Cy grunted again. He looked across the deck at O'Rourke. Mick didn't look so bad in dinner clothes—he had them fitted tightly, and he didn't need shoulder padding.

Cy said: "What's the racket, Al? I don't fall for that one about bringing him along to get material."

I said in a hurt tone: "You don't think I can write a book?"

He swore at me. "You're too damn lazy to even scribble a bad one," he said.

Carla Sard came over to us with two cocktails. She spilled most of mine, but I got out of the way. Carla had saucer eyes, dark hair, and a nose that just escaped being snubbed. Her figure was the thing, and she knew how to move it around. She said to both of us:

"Will you take them this way—or like a sandwich?"

Dana said: "What's a sandwich way of taking them?"

She handed me mine. "Cocktail sandwich—three in succession, one in the middle." She chuckled. "My God—hasn't that reached New York yet?"

Cy looked sad. "We miss *so* much, not being close to Hollywood," he said.

I tasted the drink. Carla frowned at Cy and looked at me.

"Like it?" she asked.

I nodded. "If I'm all right in a few hours, I like it," I told her. "What's in it?"

She shook her head. "I keep forgetting," she replied. "Or maybe I change things around. Anyway, there's alcohol."

Cy groaned. Carla gestured toward Mick and said:

"He says he's on the wagon—does he mean it?"

I shrugged. "He might," I told her. "Mick's hard to figure."

Carla said: "Yeah?"

I qualified the statement. "Hard for *me* to figure," I said.

She flashed me a smile that looked as though it might screen nicely.

"Thanks," she said. "I'll try him."

The radio sent dance music across the deck. The yacht was above Storm King, cruising at greater speed now. It was almost dark.

I sipped the cocktail, leaned against the rail, and looked over the group seated and sprawled near the buffet and radio. Torry Jones was talking in low tones to Sonia Vreedon; there was something about the girl I liked. She had a sharp face, gray eyes that held intelligence—and a firm mouth. She'd been on the Coast much of the time, with her father. He was on some sort of a world cruise at the moment, and there was some reason why she hadn't gone along. I couldn't think of it. She spoke without making any gestures, and she was decisive in tone.

Eric Vennell was stretched in a deck chair, between Rita Velda and a gray-haired woman who talked too much and too loudly. Rita wasn't far behind her in either respect. She'd done a wisecracking book about a bootlegger who went in for culture, and it had been a best seller. She was tall and willowy—and had red hair slicked down. Her nervousness seemed to make everyone else nervous.

Don Rayne stood near a pile of cushions, talking with a chunky human whose name was Panklin. Rayne had the build of a crew man, but a year in a stockbroker's office had taken most of his last season's crew tan from his lean face.

My eyes went to Eric Vennell again. He was watching Sonia closely; at intervals he moved his head to speak with one of the two women beside him, but his eyes always returned to Ben Vreedon's daughter. I was thinking:

They might do well together—Vennell and Sonia Vreedon. Both of them quick, hard, and sharp. One a big-league gambler, wealthy and tricky. The other the daughter of the best criminal lawyer on the Coast. A man that licked Fallon when he was at the peak—

Cy Dana interrupted my thoughts. He spoke in a low voice.

"Funny—this crowd."

I said: "Why funny?"

Dana shrugged. He tapped his mustache. There was a burst of laughter from a young group near the buffet.

"Vennell hasn't had the yacht on the Hudson for years. He never went in much for this sort of thing."

I said: "What sort of thing?"

The sportswriter said: "Crew."

I looked at Vennell and caught him watching Sonia again. His expression was intense.

"He's a yachtsman," I pointed out. "It's a big race—and a chance for a big party."

Dana said grimly: "Just between two newshounds—why is he throwing a party? What's *he* got to celebrate?"

I passed Cy a cigarette and we lighted up. I said softly: "You know something."

Cy smiled a little. "And I'm not holding it back—the way you are."

I pulled on the cigarette and watched Carla Sard move toward Mick O'Rourke, with a 'Regatta' held high. Cy said:

"I've got an apartment with Tracy, you see. He works the Street. Vennell lost a couple of million in a couple of months. He's so pleased that he's throwing a party for a mixed crowd—and he doesn't know most of them any too well."

I said: "Perhaps a farewell party."

Cy smiled a little grimly. "Does Vennell strike you like that sort of a human?" he asked.

I looked toward the yacht owner and caught him speaking to Rita Velda and staring at Sonia Vreedon. His face was relaxed, but his body was tense.

I said: "Not exactly. What, then? Here we are. The yacht's moving. Tomorrow there's the Regatta."

Cy said: "Yeah. And how come he went out of his way to get you aboard? And me?"

"Easy," I replied. "He knows I'm not a spot writer. I get a chance to read what all the other boys write, and then soliloquize on why Columbia finished second. I can do it just as well here. I've known Vennell for some years."

Cy Dana smiled. "All right," he agreed. "So have I. But this is the first year I haven't ridden the observation train."

Carla Sard came over and gestured toward Mick O'Rourke.

"The big fellow's gone off the wagon," she said triumphantly.

I grinned. "You've got a way," I said, and watched Mick toss liquid overboard, with Carla's back turned to him.

She smiled and went toward Vennell, who rose from his deck chair. Cy Dana looked at Mick and said in a mocking tone:

"And you brought *him* along just because he's a funny guy, and you couldn't be interrupted in your material digging."

I said: "That's it, Cy."

The sportswriter grunted. "It's a swell layout," he said. "But there's something wrong."

"What?" I asked innocently.

Cy started to say something, but Vennell held up a hand and looked around at the gathering.

"Dinner in the main saloon," he announced. "You may choose partners. Miss Vreedon is already chosen—the commander's honor, you know."

I looked at Cy and saw that he was not smiling. Sonia Vreedon seemed a little startled. The men started to move about a bit. Mick O'Rourke's big feet made sudden sound. He went close to Carla Sard and said boomingly:

"I'll take you, kid!"

There was sudden silence. Torry Jones stared at Mick and said:

"Sorry, big boy—she's been tooked."

Mick stopped grinning and dropped his head forward on his shoulder.

"Yeah?" he said.

Vennell looked past O'Rourke, at me. There was an amused expression in his eyes. Cy Dana said:

"Oh, God—"

"It's this way, Mick," I said, and tried to wink at the group beyond him, "Mr. Jones is an old acquaintance of Miss Sard."

The big fellow nodded his head. His body relaxed slightly.

"That makes it easier for me, huh?" he said.

Torry didn't like the laugh that got. He looked at me and said grimly:

"It'll be a hell of a book you'll write on this guy, Al."

I just smiled. Mick said slowly:

"The thing is—do you feed with me, kid—or with him?"

Carla Sard laughed lightly. She said: "Toss a coin—how's that?"

Mick nodded and reached into his pocket. He produced

a quarter that I'd seen several times before. It was a clever piece of metal splitting—tails on both sides. He tossed it to me.

Torry said: "Heads."

That made it easier. I flipped it up and watched it spin. There was a nice ring when it hit the deck. We crowded around. I said:

"Tails, boys."

Mick picked up the coin and grinned at Carla.

"I win," he said, and made a grab for her arm.

Torry looked at me and shrugged. "He *would,*" he said bitterly.

I nodded. "Sure," I agreed. "Mick's lucky like that."

Vennell and Sonia led the way toward the cabin aft. Mick O'Rourke and Carla followed. Cy Dana said very softly:

"Your big boy sticks pretty close to Vennell, eh?"

I pretended I didn't hear that. Torry called out to Carla:

"What is this thing—called love?"

Mick twisted his big head and looked serious.

"On that the better poets disagree," he said. "In its pure form it is often an elusive quality, scarcely definable."

He went into the cabin with Carla. Torry Jones sat down in a chair and held his head in both hands. He stared at me blankly. I said:

"Now you know."

Torry groaned. The yacht rolled just a little. The others paired off and followed toward the dining saloon. Cy Dana skipped his cigarette over the side. A faint odor of onions reached us, aft.

·2·

BUSINESS CARD

When the *Virgin* passed West Point, we were lying round on deck, sipping liquors and coffee, and feeling pretty comfortable. Mick O'Rourke was sprawled near me, on a half-dozen cushions. Most of the others had deck chairs. Carla turned her saucer eyes toward gray, stern buldings, clear in the light of a crescent moon, and sighed heavily. She broke a momentary silence.

"He was an honor man, and little Carla was very, very young," she said. "He'd been studying too hard—tactics, I think. I made a sweet retreat."

Torry said grimly, arms flung over his head:

"In disorder, Carla?"

Rita Velda laughed in her thinnish way. "Was this before the war, dear?" she asked nastily.

Carla made a grimace. "Even my first campaign doesn't date back *that* far," she said. "It was at high school—and Pershing had returned from France."

Rita had a coughing spell, and Carla narrowed her big eyes a little.

"Then there was the conquest at State," she said slowly, thoughtfully.

Rita said: "There's *always* a conquest at State, Carla."

"And then the Broadway battles—and the attack on Hollywood," Carla went on.

Torry Jones said lazily: "Hollywood was a major offensive, wasn't it?"

Rita Velda said sharply: "Not major—just offensive."

Eric Vennell's eyes were on Sonia Vreedon again; it seemed that each time I looked at him, he was watching the girl.

West Point was sliding aft of us. Carla sat up a little and said:

"Hollywood's swell."

Torry grinned at her. "You licked the town," he said in an admiring tone. "That makes you sweller."

Rita Velda took her cigarette from between lips that were unrouged, tapped her red hair with long fingers of her other hand.

"Virtue triumphant!" she said.

Carla sat up straight, and her lips got set in a narrow line. Then they quivered a little. She cracked a palm against the wood of her deck chair and said harshly:

"Listen, louse—you shut up."

Eric Vennell spoke quietly.

"Now, now!"

Mick O'Rourke chuckled suddenly, moved his angled knees until they touched as he lay on his broad back, and said huskily:

"The four all in the corner pocket! Nothing like calling your shots."

Rita said: "I'm sorry—you misunderstood me, dear."

Carla Sard stood up and struck a pose that wasn't at all bad to look at. She nodded her head.

"Sure," she agreed. "And I don't want to do it again."

Her voice was knife-edged. I looked at Rita, saw her shrug. Eric Vennell said cheerfully:

"Pulling for California to cross the finish line first, aren't you, Sonia?"

Sonia Vreedon took her gray eyes away from those of Rita Velda and nodded toward Vennell.

"Naturally," she said firmly. "Tim's pulling in the Number Seven rig."

Mick sat up and looked at Sonia as though he were seeing her for the first time.

"What I want to know," he said, "is are them oars they paddle with heavy?"

Torry groaned. Cy Dana said: "They get heavy—along about the last half-mile."

Mick asked slowly: "What's this guy Tim get, if he wins? What's his end of the deal?"

Vennell spoke in a peculiar tone. "He gets Sonia, for one thing."

I was watching her closely. Her eyes met Vennell's; they held a flickering expression I couldn't figure.

Cy Dana, on my right, muttered half-aloud:

"So *that's* it."

Mick O'Rourke asked slowly: "Well, that's something. What's he get if he loses?"

Don Rayne spoke from some spot near a ventilator. He said with feeling:

"Hell—from the coach."

Cy Dana muttered again: "So *that's* it!"

I turned my head a little and saw that the sportswriter was tapping his mustache and smiling.

"That's *what?*" I asked.

Cy said slowly and in a soft voice: "'What's his end of the deal?'"

His imitation of Mick's tone was not so bad. I looked stupidly at him.

"Got him sized up, eh?" I asked.

Cy shook his head. The others were talking about crew; Vennell had succeeded in getting Carla and Rita orally separated.

Cy shrugged. "Better come through, Al," he said. "You're sitting closer to Vennell than I am. We're on this boat for a reason—and some others are on her for a reason."

"Sure," I said. "To see California grab off the varsity race. To do some quiet drinking. To be sociable."

Cy grinned. "Vennell drops a few million on the Street—and wants to be sociable," he said with sarcasm. "To make sure about it he takes aboard a woman he can't keep his eyes off, but who's in love with Burke, Number Seven in the California shell. And two newspaper men he knows from experience will grab anything that looks like news. And an actress and a she-writer who hate each other."

I pulled my chair a bit closer to Dana's. He had a sharp eye, but he'd left out something important.

"And what else?" I asked.

He stopped grinning at me. "And this big bruiser, O'Rourke," he said. "With you trying to pass him off as a funny guy you're working for material."

I said nothing. There was a lull in the conversation and the gray-haired woman whose name I'd forgotten said suddenly:

"Mr. Vennell—won't you tell us how the yacht got her name?"

Carla had her back turned to Rita Velda; she was leaning against the rail, looking toward the fading West Point buildings. She faced about now.

"Yes, do," she said, smiling at Vennell.

He nodded. "It isn't as bad as you think," he said. "There was a slipup at the launching—and we didn't have champagne. We didn't have anything strong, as a matter of fact. So one of the workers dug up a milk bottle—half filled. I smashed that across her prow and called her the *Virgin*."

There were varied comments. Cy Dana got his head close to mine and said:

"Know the other story?"

I shook my head. Cy said slowly: "Maybe if I tell

you enough, you'll come through with the truth about the big fellow."

I said: "Maybe."

Cy spoke very softly; the others were talking about yachts.

"The one I heard was that eight or ten years ago Vennell had a bad reputation on the big Atlantic boats. He handled cards smoothly, when there was big money up. There was a scene one night, in the card room of one of the big girls, and the first officer came down to see him, in his cabin. He must have said some nasty things to Vennell. There was a fight, and the first officer went down. He didn't get up."

I widened eyes on Cy's. He smiled as though he were talking about something unimportant.

"The officer died, and there was a pretty mess. Vennell got out of it, but it was a job. A year or so later he got going on the Street—speculation. Then he got this yacht. Ever notice the crew?"

I shook my head. Cy said: "Well, there's no first officer—no first mate."

I said: "She may not be big enough."

Cy said: "She is. She rates a first mate, but she's never had one. He swore no boat of his ever *would* have one. And that's why he called her the *Virgin*."

I said slowly: "Because she hasn't had her first mate—"

Cy lighted a cigarette. "That's it," he said.

I yawned. "And you believe it?"

He pulled on the cigarette. "It's a damn sight better than the one about the milk bottle," he said. "And I've checked up on part of it. He did kill a liner's first officer."

"Well," I said, "you think it's a funny layout. You don't like the way things look. What's going to happen?"

Cy Dana swore at me. "Did he tell that roughneck you brought aboard what he was supposed to do?"

I looked toward the nearest shore. "It should be good weather for the races," I said.

Cy Dana regarded his cigarette and nodded his head very slowly.

"All right, Al," he said. "You work it your way. But when things break, I'll scoop hell out of you."

I laughed at him. "*If* they break, and if there were any such thing as a scoop," I corrected.

He smiled with his eyes grim. "We haven't got leg-men on yachts," he reminded. "Or cops ready to tip off their pet newshound. I did police work before I got into the sport end."

I nodded. "I did it before I decided to steal two or three other guys' styles and get myself a column," I replied. "This just looks like a nice quiet party to me."

Cy Dana closed his eyes. Carla's voice rose very suddenly, sharp and clear.

"Some day you'll get a knife stuck in your back, Rita!" she said.

Mick O'Rourke kicked my chair with one of his big feet and winked at me.

Rita Velda said calmly: "You're *so* sensitive, my dear."

A glass crashed. I sat up straight and watched Carla face the writer, her eyes narrowed with rage. She said excitedly:

"Either you'll get off this yacht—or I will!"

Torry Jones got to his feet. He was a little shaky on them. I looked at three empty, tall glasses near his chair. He said thickly:

"Want me to put her ashore, Carla?"

Carla's hating eyes held a peculiar smile now. She nodded her head.

"Chuck her over, Torry," she said.

Torry Jones moved toward Rita, who regarded him with contempt. She said slowly:

"You don't drink as well as you fly."

Torry was almost at her side when Mick O'Rourke got to his feet. He was watching the flier closely. Eric Vennell was smiling with his lips.

"Careful, Torry," he warned. "Don't be foolish."

The flier was tight. He chuckled toward Rita, who stood close to the yacht rail, watching him. He said:

"Can you swim?"

Rita spoke. "Sit down and tell us how you flew over and under clouds—again," she said. "I haven't heard it since Van Dane's party the other night."

It was the wrong thing to say to Torry Jones, and Rita realized that right away. He sobered up just enough to stop being funny and to get mad. He said:

"Over you go!"

He had her in his arms when three of us got moving. Vennell was the nearest to them, but Mick O'Rourke moved with greater speed. I was calling out sharply when his form moved past me. For a second his big back blotted out my sight of Rita and Torry.

Then Rita was shoved to one side; Vennell caught her in his arms. The figure of Torry Jones rose from the deck, arms swinging. Mick O'Rourke gritted:

"Here's your—chaser!"

Torry's body shot over the rail, twisting. Carla Sard screamed shrilly; Vennell swore in a low, harsh voice.

Sonia Vreedon's voice reached me above the babble.

"The propeller—"

Cy Dana said grimly: "He can swim, I suppose. We're aft—no danger from the propeller."

We were at the rail now, all except Eric Vennell. He was running toward the bridge, and calling in a sharp voice:

"Heads up—man overboard!"

Mick O'Rourke looked at me and grinned. He seemed pretty pleased. I said:

"You damn fool—what did you do that for?"

The big fellow kept on grinning. The yacht started to swing wide, to get around in a circle. The siren wailed three times, in short sound. I caught a glimpse of Torry Jone's head—and an arm moving.

Carla Sard was beside me, but she wasn't paying any attention to me. She was very excited, and pounded at Mick's big chest with tiny, clenched fists.

"You've killed him! You've drowned him!" she shrilled. "Murderer!"

Mick laughed at her. "If he can't swim, what'd he fly the Atlantic for?" he said.

The yacht was coming around nicely. The siren wailed again. There was a faint jangle of bells and the engine vibration became less noticeable. The speed was slower.

Some of the group moved toward the prow of the craft. Carla Sard staggered dramatically toward a deck chair and collapsed into it. There was light on the water, from moon and stars, and a searchlight beam shot downward from the bridge. It caught the figure of Torry. He seemed to be sprawling around a lot.

Sonia Vreedon said calmly: "He can't swim *much*, that's sure."

Carla heard her and cried shrilly: "He's killed him! He's killed—Torry—"

Cy Dana said: "Don't yelp so much—you're not on the set."

A voice bawled from the bridge: "We're tossing down a line—"

Then Carla was speaking again. She'd stopped being dramatic and was just hard.

"Listen, you sports hound!" she snapped at Cy. "Don't talk that way to me!"

Cy stared at her. There was a great deal of excitement on the yacht, but Carla had forgotten about that. She forgot about one thing very quickly, if another annoyed her.

I said: "Torry's in bad shape."

He was splashing a lot, and the yacht was still a few hundred yards distant. Carla didn't seem to care.

"This is the hell of a party!" she said. "I'm telling you that!"

"You mean Carla likes Jones?" he said, and his tone was hurt.

Vennell stared at him. He sat up a little; said sharply:

"Listen, big fellow—this is a job for *you*. You stop being so damn social and use your eyes!"

I grinned. "Mick's fallen for Carla," I said. "He'll be stroking her hair when the shots pop—and you take the tumble, Eric."

It seemed to me that I was kidding, but Vennell didn't take it that way. His lean face got hard, and his gray eyes cold. He stood up and faced me.

"It isn't that funny, Al," he said. "I'm on the spot. When a lot of humans were losing money on the Street, *I* was making money. They didn't like it, because it was their money I was making. This is quiet talk, see—it goes for you and the big fellow."

I said. "What did they care about *you* making money? How did they know—"

Vennell smiled a little. "I was the dummy partner in a certain firm," he said. "My idea was that nobody knew it—that counted. They didn't, until they dropped a lot of money. Then they found out."

I said: "Why?"

Vennell looked at Mick O'Rourke. He spoke in a low voice.

"Because they weren't accustomed to losing big money," he said. "One of the firm slipped up. They took the wrong sort of money. Racket coin, from a gang. An important gang. The money was lost, and they found out I was the big man in the firm. So they came to me, with suggestions. I said no."

Mick O'Rourke was staring at Vennell. He said very softly:

"You lost gangster money—and you won't pay the boys back. So they put you on the spot."

Vennell said: "That's it. I got up this party in a hurry—

the yacht was down on Long Island. The Regatta was coming up. I figured I'd be safer aboard her, on the Hudson, than about anywhere else. I wanted someone around, even here. So I told Al to dig up a good man. He got you, Mick."

"Yeah." Mick's voice was peculiar in tone. "Sure."

I didn't say anything. Mick got up and found a cigarette. Vennell said:

"I wanted a lively crowd, to take my mind off things. But I don't want any killings on the yacht."

Mick chuckled. "I thought he could swim," he said.

Vennell said: "Torry'll hate you for that, Mick."

The engine of the yacht made a steady throb. Faint sound of music drifted down to us. There was the lap and swish of water against the craft's sides. Mick grunted.

"I can laugh him out of it," he said.

Vennell shook his head. "Torry's no dub," he replied. "It takes nerve to fly the Atlantic, and he did it. You made a fool of him, and the woman he liked was there to see it. That won't help."

Mick said: "I'm sorry."

Vennell shrugged. "Watch yourself and take things easy. Maybe the *Virgin* got away without being spotted. But she'll be spotted at Poughkeepsie. We'll arrive in a few hours now. You've got to keep your eyes open."

Mick said: "Can you give me some names? It might make it easier."

The yacht owner shook his head. "That wouldn't help," he said. "I don't want trouble. It may not come. I don't want any of my guests hurt. That's an angle they might work, to scare me."

I nodded. "That's more like it," I said. "If they kill you—that wouldn't get their coin back. But if they scare you—"

Vennell said sharply: "They won't." He looked at Mick O'Rourke, who was standing near the door, his eyes half-closed.

"Cut the love stuff and remember I paid you five grand," he said. "Just because things don't seem very tough, that doesn't mean they won't *get* that way."

Mick opened his eyes and nodded. "Sure," he agreed. "That's why a gun makes so much noise—because it's quiet just before."

Vennell smiled a little. He said: "And if you go overboard again—keep your pants on. Miss Sard complained."

The big fellow chuckled. Vennell went to the door and half opened it.

"I'll try to calm Torry, so that he won't hurt you," he said.

Mick nodded. "Fix it right," he said. "Tell him I'll slip him a grand if he lays off me."

Vennell smiled a little grimly and went outside. He closed the door behind him, and his footfalls sounded more faintly as he moved along the corridor. Mick sat in the chair again and watched me thoughtfully. I looked at the suite's ceiling, frowning. After a while I said:

"Well, Vennell's getting old. That was a rotten story."

Mick nodded. "Lousy," he said.

"The reason he gave for being put on the spot wasn't so bad," I muttered. "But the idea of figuring this sort of a party as a way to keep clear of guns, that's cold."

Mick said, grinning: "Dumb."

I said: "Cy Dana's wise to the fact that I didn't just bring you along because you're funny, Mick. Be a little careful when he's around."

The big fellow nodded. He got up and said suddenly: "I gotta go up and apologize to Miss Sard."

I grinned at him. "That'll be difficult," I said. "How'll you put it?"

He said: "I might tell her I was thinkin' about other things."

"Not bad," I agreed. "You saved Torry's life."

Mick O'Rourke swore. "He won't remember that so much," he said.

I narrowed my eyes. "Why not?"

Mick smiled a little. "There's the crack in the jaw I had to give him—in the water," he said.

I stared at the big fellow. "You did that?" I muttered. "Why?"

Mick said in surprise: "He was drowning, wasn't he?"

I waited a few seconds. "*Was* he?" I asked in a hard tone.

There was a little silence while Mick looked for an ashtray and found it.

"Sure," he replied finally. "I read about it in a book. You always have to soak 'em in the jaw when you go in after 'em like that."

I whistled softly. "And you remembered that *before* you made the dive, eh?"

Mick O'Rourke raised his big arms and touched the suite's ceiling. He yawned noisily.

"Yeah," he said. "I'm funny that way."

3

It was almost midnight when the *Virgin* slid past gaily decorated craft, siren wailing a salute toward Poughkeepsie, the boathouses of the crews, and Highlands. I'd run out of cigarettes; things were fairly quiet on deck, and I went to get some. Mick O'Rourke was talking to Don Rayne; Carla Sard was giving him the cold shoulder, and most of the others were at the rails, watching the shore and other boats. Torry Jones was not on deck.

I got the cigarettes, went along the corridor from the suite, into the smoke room. It was a small room, done in mission style and lighted dully. Almost the first thing I saw was the card lying near a table, on the floor. It was the usual oblong name card, and the side that faced my eyes as I stood over it held very regular, perfect writing. The ink was reddish in color—the name Albert Connors was at the upper left corner.

I leaned down and picked up the card. I read very slowly, but easily:

"Albert Connors—runs column in *News*. Medium-sized, dark hair and eyes. Nose slightly large. Acquainted with V. And others, many. Lies well. Suite B with M. O'R. Stalling on O'R. Watch after V. gets works."

That was all. It was very precise and clear. The description of me was good enough. I was acquainted with Vennell, and it was possible that I lied well. That was part of a columnist's job. I occupied Suite B with Mick, and I was stalling about him. I was to be watched, after Vennell "gets works."

I swore a little and turned the card over. I read in printing of various sizes:

"Henry McFarren—Leather Goods—1217 Garrick Avenue—Crissville, Wyoming."

The card was very new in appearance. I turned it over again, sucked on my cigarette, and read the perfect, round writing. When I got through, I went over to a small mirror and looked at my nose. It was slightly large.

There was sound behind me; Griggs entered the smoke room, his poker face turned toward mine.

"Is there something I can do, Mr. Connors?" he asked quietly.

I slipped the card into my pocket and said: "No, thanks. Nothing."

He nodded, smiling mechanically, went over to one of the tables and straightened out a matchbox, looked momentarily toward a spot on the floor. It seemed to me that it was the spot from which I had lifted the card, but I could not be positive. In the corridor his footfalls died.

I got the card from my pocket and read it the third time. It hadn't changed any, and it meant about the same thing.

Three or four voices came to me, repeating in hoarse unison:

"California—California—CALIFORNIA!"

From the deck above there were cheers, some of them feminine in tone. A launch screeched sound in the distance. The *Virgin's* siren wailed several times. Up the river somewhere there was the dull report of what might have been a cannon.

I got the card back in a pocket again and went slowly from the smoke room. When I reached the deck, the yacht was opposite the California boathouse, and well out in the Hudson. The searchlight beam brought out the letters of the college, painted raggedly on the sloping roof, clearly. The yacht was barely moving—there was the rattle of the anchor chain.

Torry Jones brushed close to me as I walked aft. He was frowning. He said:

"You'd better be careful, Al. I'll pull a fast one on that bruiser of yours."

I smiled. "I've almost got all the material from him that I need," I said. "The rest I can get in the death house."

Torry said: "What do you mean, death house?"

I shrugged. "That's where they'll put *him,* after *you* try to pull a fast one."

The flier caught my arm as I started to move on. He said:

"Ever see a bomber come down in a crash—one of the big, tri-motored girls?"

I shook my head. Torry said grimly: "They fall harder than the small ones."

I nodded. "Variation on an old theme," I said. "But do they fall as often?"

Torry swore. "He won't get anywhere with Carla," he said. "She's not a roughneck."

I thought that over. "You might be right," I said, with a lot of doubt in my voice.

He was getting mad. His voice showed it when he said:

"I've got an idea that Vennell brought that guy on board to show me up."

I said: "Don't be childish, Torry. Vennell isn't interested in Carla."

He said: "No? Then what's O'Rourke here for? That line of yours doesn't go with me."

I shrugged. "You mentioned that before," I told him. "The thing that counts is that Mick's here, that you got funny with Rita Velda because you'd had too much to drink, and that he threw you overboard. Even at that—he pulled you out."

Torry said: "Damn him—he knocked me unconscious doing it!"

I stared at him. "No?" I said. Then I changed my tone. "Well, you were probably pulling him down."

The flier smiled; it was the sort of smile that wasn't particularly happy.

"That's *his* story," he said. "But I'll bet he figured on the crack in the jaw before he jumped."

I made a clicking sound. "That isn't like Mick," I said sadly. "You misjudge him."

He swore at me and moved along. I went aft and said to Mick:

"You've got the keys of that small hunk of luggage. Go down and find them, will you?"

The big fellow blinked at me. "I ain't got no keys," he said.

I smiled at him. "Yes you have, Mick," I said. "Go down and think it over."

Light dawned in his eyes. He grinned at Don Rayne and moved away. The last-season stroke of Columbia winked at me.

"He's a likable dumbbell," he said.

I grinned at Rayne. "Most dumbbells are likable," I said.

It took a little hunting to find Vennell. I discovered him on the bridge, and we went to Suite B together. Mick was sitting on his bed and grinning. He said:

"You had me winging with that key stuff, until I wised up."

I closed the door and locked it. Then I handed Eric Vennell the card.

"Found it in the smoke room, on the floor," I said. "Nothing else. It's about you, Mick, and me."

Eric Vennell read the writing, his gray eyes narrowing, and his lips getting tight. When he finished, he read it again. Then he looked at me and said:

"Good—God!"

He went to the nearest wicker and sat down heavily. Mick O'Rourke got up and looked at me questioningly. I took the card from Vennell's fingers and handed it to Mick. He read it three or four times, his lips moving. He started to hand it back to me, then he read it again. Then he said very slowly:

"Yeah—sure."

Vennell said tonelessly: "Yeah—sure—what?"

Mick rubbed his thick lips with the back of a big hand. He made a swift movement and looked down at his snub-nosed gun. The sight of it seemed to cheer him. He got it out of sight.

"It may be—a joke," he said slowly.

Eric Vennell stared at me. "I'm slated—to get the works," he said heavily.

I smiled. "And it's bulletined by a dropped card," I said.

Vennell got up from the chair and paced back and forth, his shoulders sagging a little.

"Just the same—I'm marked, spotted," he said thickly. "That card wasn't meant to be dropped, or else someone's so sure I can't wriggle clear—"

Mick O'Rourke spoke thoughtfully: "That's pretty writin'—for a killin' guy."

I nodded. "Almost like a woman's writing," I said.

Vennell faced me. "A woman's—"

He checked his words, started pacing back and forth again. Mick O'Rourke looked at me and said very softly:

"He's been alone a lot—on board."

Vennell swung around. "They don't want to finish me—not yet. They want money. The money they lost on the Street. They're trying to get at me—"

I said: "Well, you know everyone on board, Eric. You picked them."

Vennell smiled grimly. "The crew is all right," he said. "Same crew I've always had. All right, so far as I know. And I picked the guests, certainly. But I didn't pick them for—"

He stopped again. I said: "For pleasure. You picked them to keep your mind off this thing."

Vennell shrugged. I took the card from Mick and turned it over. I said:

"Crissville, Wyoming."

There was the whistle of a launch. Music drifted to us as the boat passed the *Virgin*. Voices reached the yacht—there were cheers for Washington. Someone apparently spotted Don Rayne. There were shouts up to him—his voice called back.

Eric Vennell said grimly: "You've got to stick close to me, O'Rourke. This is getting me."

Mick nodded. "Sure," he said. "If they slam you down, I'll be right on top of 'em."

Vennell swore. "That'll help me a lot!" he muttered.

Mick said: "Well—I can't shoot *first*, can I?"

Vennell groaned. Then suddenly he stood still, his fists clenched at his sides. He laughed bitterly.

"I'm going up on deck," he said in a fierce voice. "I'll be on deck tomorrow—yelling for California to finish first. It's bluff, that's all!"

He went to the door, unlocked it, went outside and

along the corridor. Mick looked at me. I gestured after Vennell.

"You've got a job," I reminded.

Mick said huskily: "Game guy—what's he care about gettin' murdered, with a boat race coming up?"

I smiled. "Calling card," I said grimly. "Visiting card." I slipped it into my pocket. "You believe in fairies, Mick?"

The big fellow's eyes got large. "Are there any on board?" he asked.

I groaned. "Go on up and find out," I said. "I was thinking about something else."

Mick O'Rourke grinned. "If I find any, I'll tip you off, Al," he said.

I tried a kick at his pants, and missed. He went along the corridor. Nothing much bothered Mick, not even the New York police. I sat on the edge of the wicker and listened to faint cheering, and distant boat whistles. I said, half to myself:

"It may be rough going."

And I wasn't thinking about the varsity race.

•3•

SUITE AFFAIR

There were clouds crossing the crescent moon when I went on deck; there was dancing aft, to music from Villa Vallee, in New York. I stood near the rail, on the port side, and looked at the boathouses of the different crews. While I was doing it, Don Rayne came along, pulling on an upside-down pipe. He stopped near me and squinted his blue eyes toward the west shore of the Hudson.

''Damn!'' he breathed. ''I'd like to be over there—out there tomorrow with my fingers around wood!''

I nodded sympathetically. ''But you'd take a licking,'' I said. ''That's not so much fun.''

He shrugged. ''Columbia might fool them,'' he said. ''She's got a green crew, but they're strong. And Phelps is the best coach of the lot.''

I said: ''The odds are around three to one against her. California's shell is loaded with veterans. Babe Harron stroked them to win last year. He's strong as an ox—and when he pulls an oar—the others pull.''

Rayne nodded. ''Harron's the best man—and Tim Burke's right ahead of him. They've got power. Little Ed Dale's got a head; he can step up the beat—and get it. But things happen that even the best coxswain can't handle.''

I smiled. ''What?'' I said. ''California's got a rough-water crew, and they can row in the dark. No false starts this year.''

The former stroke shrugged his broad shoulders. His eyes were half-closed on the painted roof of the California boathouse. From the opposite side of the river, from Poughkeepsie, came the tooting of auto horns, faint cheering.

''Cal and Columbia aren't the only crews in the big race,'' Rayne said. ''There's Washington and Navy. And Pennsylvania. And the others. There might be a surprise.''

I grinned. ''California—by three lengths,'' I prophesied. ''Then Columbia, fighting it out with Penn. Navy and Washington close up, with the others stringing out. Syracuse and Cornell scrapping for sixth and seventh. Wisconsin and the first Poughkeepsie shell of Dartmouth trying to keep from being last.''

Rayne took his pipe from between even teeth and inspected the bowl.

''Dartmouth might fool you,'' he said. ''They licked Yale and Harvard in the triangular regattas. Syracuse might be up ahead of Penn and Washington. But the race is between Columbia and the Golden Bears.''

I nodded. ''If you want to call it a race,'' I said. ''It'll be nice for Sonia Vreedon.''

His eyes were sharp on mine. ''Why?'' he asked, and his tone was strangely hard.

I said: ''Well—Tim Burke's pulling in Number Seven's rig—for California.''

Rayne smiled a little and said: ''Oh, yeah—that's right.''

I said: ''They're both from California. Her father's a big criminal lawyer out there.''

Rayne said quietly: ''I've heard about him.''

He got his pipe back between his teeth again, giving

me the idea that he knew something he wasn't telling me about. Then he grinned at me.

"Think I'll turn in," he said. "Want to be up early. Going over to my old boathouse tomorrow, to see the boys."

I nodded and said good-night to him. He went away. I stood looking toward the boathouses. They were dark, most of them—no lights showing. A few of the crews were bedding in Poughkeepsie hotels, but most of them were in the boathouses, in special quarters. It seemed to me that the water was roughing up a bit; there was more wind now. The moon was under cloud, and few stars showed. The night had got much darker.

I walked aft and saw Vennell sipping a tall-glassed drink and talking to Rita Velda. Mick O'Rourke was sprawled in a deck chair, not far distant. His eyes were not wide open, but they moved about. He was looking at people.

I paused near Vennell and the she-scribbler. She was saying:

"But Genoa—I thought it was lousy. Hot as the devil, you know. And not too clean. The French colonial towns—those are the places. Strange food, people—and yet something of Paris, my dear."

Carla Sard's voice came clearly, from some feet away:

"Oh, God—I wish I was in Agua Caliente! *There's* a spot."

Vennell's fingers were twisting a little, at his sides. Rita moved a lean leg and paid no attention to the picture gal.

"Silkworm salad," she said. "Shark's fins, garnished with baked cuttlefish heads and served with bits of marvelous dried fish."

Mick O'Rourke sat up and said: "Is the beer good over there?"

Carla Sard laughed harshly and then remembered that she wasn't supposed to be amused at Mick. She frowned at him. I looked around for Torry Jones and didn't see him. Cold towels on his injured jaw, I thought.

Rita said: "Seaweed jam, for dessert. And did you ever try the African *mwambe*?"

Eric Vennell smiled apologetically. Mick O'Rourke said:

"Can you get it up in Harlem?"

Rita looked at him with contempt. Then she said to Eric and me:

"Chicken, fried in palm oil."

Mick groaned. Carla said in a loud tone, addressing Cy Dana:

"You mustn't steal her stuff for your sporting column, Cy."

Rita sighed. "And *m'poss,*" she said, or something like that. "Pudding of pumpkin seeds and the larvæ of white worms—"

Mick O'Rourke groaned. "I'll stick to the Brass Rail," he announced. "I only got worms once there—"

I said: "All right, Mick—but Miss Velda has traveled."

Carla spoke softly to Cy Dana. "Lovely things—travel books. One learns so much about places, people—and foods."

Rita turned away from Eric Vennell and faced the picture gal. Then she shrugged.

"I'll go to bed," she said. "If I can find my cabin."

Eric Vennell smiled. "I'll go along with you," he said. "It isn't far—"

He stopped suddenly. Mick O'Rourke got to his feet and said:

"Mind if I come with you two? I haven't seen much of this boat."

Vennell looked relieved. I caught Cy Dana's eyes on mine, grimly amused. Carla Sard said nastily:

"Bring him back with you, Eric."

Rita nodded. "I'll see to that," she said. "And I won't let him throw Torry overboard again."

She followed Vennell along the deck, with Mick behind her. Carla looked about the thinning group and said bitterly:

"I *still* think she's a louse."

Cy Dana frowned. "You're shocking, Carla," he said. "You've stayed in Hollywood too long."

The picture gal smiled. "The town would do Rita some good," she returned. "It gives highbrows a sense of humor."

"Or a pain in the neck," I said.

Carla stared at me. "Lord! You, too?" she breathed. "You're all agin me."

Cy grinned. "You've got Torry—when he's aboard the ship."

I watched anger get into Carla's eyes. The yacht bells sounded one o'clock.

"I'm bored," she said, and stretched arms that were nice to see. "I shouldn't have come along."

Cy said: "It'll be a sweet race. The varsity is always something to watch. The thing has rhythm."

I said: "It's only three days or so—on the yacht, Carla. You can get ashore tomorrow, into Poughkeepsie."

The picture gal widened her saucer eyes. "Poughkeepsie!" she said in a stricken tone. "Oh, God!"

2

I couldn't sleep. The chances were that I'd had not enough to drink, or that what I'd had had been too good. I woke Mick up, looking at my watch with the lights switched on. It was after three, and the *Virgin* had motion.

"Going to be rough," I said. "All the simpler for the California shell."

Mick looked at me with sleepy eyes. It wasn't too cool in the cabin; his pajamas—purple, with great yellow slashes—made him look like a giant out of the pages of a brat's book.

"I can stand gettin' sick—for five grand," he muttered sleepily. "What's your cut, Al? For thinking of me?"

"About three grand," I said.

That woke him up. "Hell!" he breathed, sitting up in the bed. "*You* ain't taking chances of being shot."

I grinned at him. "I've got to think of my public," I said. "I'm on the yacht."

Mick grunted. "You know what *I* use your sheet for," he muttered.

I frowned at him. "Your Rabelaisian humor is pretty stiff for this cruise," I said.

He blinked at me. "My what?" he said.

I swung bare feet to the floor and got into slippers. Then I looked at him and thought of something that I wanted to say and was afraid of saying. I said it.

"Mick—you're playing straight in this deal?"

He looked hurt. "What do you mean?" he said.

I smiled at him. "Vennell's worried about something," I said. "He isn't just a good actor. He expects something to happen. He's lied to us, but that doesn't mean there isn't something wrong. You were pretty close to Joe Daltos, before he went to Germany for a bad stomach."

The big fellow stared at me. "Forget it," he said. "Joe didn't lose any coin on the Street. And if he did—he wouldn't whine to get it back."

I said: "All right, Mick—that's all I wanted to know. It wouldn't have been so funny if I'd got you aboard and you were thinking more about some other fellow than about Vennell."

Mick dropped back on the sheet and chuckled. He acted as if he really thought my idea was funny.

"Can you figure that?" he breathed. "You thinking

that maybe you'd put aboard a gun waitin' for the chance to get Vennell!''

I said slowly: ''I hadn't seen you for a few weeks, Mick. You never can tell.''

He sat up and pointed a big finger at me. ''You cut that line out!'' he growled. ''I play square—one way or the other.''

I grinned. ''That's swell.'' I said. ''I feel better.''

I got a pair of flannels from a bag, and a white shirt. When I stood up to put them on Mick said:

''Going for a swim?''

I shook my head. ''Just a walk around the deck.''

Mick grunted. ''Want me along?'' he asked.

I shook my head. ''Your feet make too much noise,'' I said.

As I went outside, closing the door behind me, I heard Mick O'Rourke chuckling. The corridor was lighted dully; I got to deck the quickest way, and quietly. There was little light up above; I came out forward. A freight train was rumbling along the west shore, over or close to the tracks on which the observation train would run during the races. I went to the rail and watched it. A cool wind was blowing; the water was rough.

When the voices reached me, I stood very still and tried to place them. They were very soft and reached me only at intervals. The wind was off the bow, and I judged that the speakers were somehwere aft. It sounded as though they were on the deck below, but I couldn't be sure.

It went on for some time; then I moved slowly aft. There were only a few hooded lights on deck; no one was about. The space aft, where the group had danced and drunk, held empty deck chairs. I stood near one, waited. After a few seconds the voices reached me again. They were pitched below normal tones, had a monotonous quality.

They came from the deck below, and farther aft. There

were intervals of ten or fifteen seconds when I heard nothing. The wind made sounds in the rigging of the *Virgin;* that made it more difficult.

There was a companionway on the starboard side: I found it and tiptoed toward the steps. I had almost reached them when the first scream shrilled with the wind. I stood motionlessly. There was another scream.

Almost instantly there was a crashing sound. The screams and the crash came from some spot in the cabin section, forward and below. I drew in a deep breath, waited. A voice very close to me said:

"Please—Tim—"

There was the sound of a splash, not too loud, but louder than the breaking of waves against the ship. And there were other splashes—easily recognized. The stroking of arms in water; the foot kick of a swimmer.

At the foot of the companionway there was a blur of color in the darkness, the quick breathing of a human being. From somewhere forward a voice called:

"What's—the matter?"

I recognized that voice; it was Don Rayne's. There were the faint sounds of people running—a door slammed. A form was at the foot of the companionway; I backed up and my body struck a small table. Something tinkled; I twisted around, grabbed for the swaying glass.

My fingernails struck it—swept it from the surface. It was no use—I was bending low, getting my shape behind a small ventilator, when the glass crashed. At the same second the figure of the woman reached the top of the companionway.

I sensed that—heard it. There was the quick intake of breath. A small exclamation, almost smothered. The yacht rolled.

The sigh that reached me showed that the woman believed the roll of the craft to have caused the glass breakage. I held my breath, kept my body motionless. A voice from forward came down on the wind.

"Doctor Bryce—get Bryce!"

There were footfalls close to my crouched figure. They died a little, and I lifted my head. The figure was dressed in black; it was the swing of the arms that I recognized. The swing brought me voice recognition; it clarified those two words.

Sonia Vreedon. And the one who had gone over the side of the yacht, from a spot close to the water—perhaps with a smooth dive—that had been Burke. Tim Burke. Number Seven in California shell.

I straightened, stood up. Sonia was out of sight. Earlier she had been dressed in something white—a dinner gown that had made her look rather good. Perhaps she had changed; perhaps the dark color was that of a wrap. Certainly she had expected Tim Burke—and had clothed herself so that there would be a better chance of her not being seen. But I had seen her.

My white shirt was conspicuous, but I had to risk that. I went hurriedly down the companionway that Sonia had ascended. The deck below was open; it was the stern of the yacht. The moon was still under cloud, but in sky spots there were breaks, and stars shone. Faint light was on the water, and in that light I could see the form of the swimmer. Brown showed as he stroked strongly. I raised my eyes. Beyond and to the right of his line of progress was the California boathouse.

For seconds I stood there, watching the white breakage of water as the swimmer moved. Then I turned toward the companionway, started up it. Something yellow lay wedged between the surface of a step and the low, slanted rail. Something yellow and folded.

I reached down; my fingers touched paper. It was folded into a neat square, and not too thick. I slipped it into a pocket of my flannels, moved to the upper deck, went forward. There had been the screams—and the slammed door. I hurried along the deck.

A voice said grimly, from one side: "Hold up, there!"

I stopped. The thickset figure of the second officer stepped around some superstructure; in his right hand was something that gleamed dully. I smiled at him.

"Hello," I said, not remembering his name. "I heard screams—what's wrong?"

He looked at my hands. He had on a bluish robe, and his gray mustache was bristly.

"Where'd you hear them from?" he asked.

I said: "Aft, at the stern."

He said: "Aft, at the stern, eh?"

I nodded. "Yeah," I replied. "I'd walked back there from a spot forward, at the bow."

He didn't smile. I stopped smiling and said:

"What happened?"

He slipped the gun into a pocket of his bluish robe. His voice was grim.

"A human got into Mr. Vennell's suite," he said.

I stared at him. "But I thought the screams were female," I said.

The second officer, nodded. I remembered that his name was Rosecrans.

"They *were* female," he replied.

I said: "Oh."

The second officer shook his head. "Not that," he stated. "Mr. Vennell woke up—and the fellow inside made a break for it. He ran into Miss Sard in the corridor."

I thought that over. "What was she doing in the corridor?" I asked.

Rosecrans grunted. "She *says* she was trying to find the deck," he stated.

A figure loomed up behind the second officer. It was Cy Dana. He stared at me.

"How'd *you* get here?" he asked.

I shrugged. "Southern Pacific to New Orleans, boat to New York—Central to Poughkeepsie."

Cy said: "It isn't funny. Someone broke into Vennell's cabin."

I corrected him. "Suite," I said. "Well, it wasn't me. I couldn't sleep and came up for some air."

Rosecrans nodded grimly. "And Miss Sard was *trying* to come up for air," he said.

I thought about Sonia Vreedon, but I didn't do anything else about her.

"A man gets about easier than a woman," I said.

The second officer spoke grimly. "It looks that way."

He moved aft, leaving Cy Dana eyeing me closely. I said:

"Well?"

He grinned. "*Maybe* it wasn't you, at that," he replied.

"Thanks," I replied. "Where were *you*?"

He grinned at me. "I've got too much brains to try a stunt like that," he said. "That pug's too big for me."

He was wearing a towelish bathrobe from which he fished cigarettes and matches. I bummed one of them.

"You mean Mick?" I said. "What's he got to do with this?"

Cy swore at me, but held a match below the tip of my cigarette. The wind blew it out and I moved closer, getting a light on the second try.

"Still stalling, eh?" Cy said. "Suppose I'll have to read the inside works in that lousy column of yours, next week." He pitched his voice high. " 'They say that Eric Vennell had a bodyguard on his aptly named yacht, the *Virgin,* during his Hudson jaunt to the shell scrap at Poughkeepsie, last week.' "

I said: "You're certainly working that idea hard, Cy."

He nodded. "The second scream pulled me out of the bed and into something. When I got outside and down the corridor, just one guy had got there ahead of me. It was O'Rourke. He had that picture lady by the arms and was trying to shake words out of her. But they didn't shake."

I nodded. "Mick likes her," I told him. "He was worried about her screaming, I guess."

Cy said: "He didn't act worried—he acted just plain sore."

I pulled on my cigarette. "She was screaming—and woke him up," I said. "Mick likes his sleep."

"And his job," Cy said harshly.

I made a clicking sound and went past Cy to the companionway that led down to the cabin deck. A lot of people were wandering around in dressing gowns, robes, and whatnot. Rita Velda stood near the door of her cabin, a twisted smile on her face. She said to me:

"That's the first time Carla hasn't got her man, isn't it?"

I smiled and went along to the turn in the corridor near Vennell's suite. I had to pass Carla's cabin; her door was half opened. She was lying on her bed, attended by two women whose names I didn't remember. There was a man standing near the door; he looked like a traveling salesman with a good appetite. It was Doctor Bryce. I asked him how she was.

He started to say that she was ill, but Carla sat up and swore at me. It startled me.

"Don't get excited," I told her. "It was just that I was being nice and—"

"He was your build!" she said in a loud voice. "He was dressed in black, with a mask over his face."

I grinned. "Jesse James, maybe," I said.

She swore at me again. The doctor spoke.

"You're upsetting her."

I went along the corridor, turned, and moved toward the entrance of Vennell's suite. Mick's voice reached me as I tapped on the door. He said:

"Yeah—who's there?"

I said: "Al."

His big feet made the usual racket as he came over and snapped a lock, opened the door. He grunted at me.

"Where *you* been all this time?" he asked.

I said: "I *haven't* been dressed in black and wearing a mask. I was on deck."

I walked past Mick and went toward Vennell. He was seated in a chair near a small desk, staring at me blankly. He said in a husky voice:

"They tried—to get me, Al!"

I stood looking down at him. "Just what happened?" I said.

He sighed. "The door was locked. I was sleeping restlessly. The clicking sound woke me up, but I didn't move. There was a gun on that table, next to the bed."

He pointed toward a small table, near the head of his bed. He went on.

"The door opened—not too much. Light from the corridor showed me the figure; my head was turned toward the fellow. He was wearing something that looked like a black robe. He had a mask that completely covered his face. He shut the door behind him and came toward the bed. I called out: 'Who's there?' His body jerked; he turned and made for the door. I reached for the gun—the door slammed. I got out of bed."

Eric Vennell shook his head slowly. "There were screams—the fellow ran into Carla in the corridor, round the corner. He grabbed her by the throat and banged her head against the wall. Then he got away."

I looked at Mick. His mouth was slightly open.

"And then you grabbed Carla by the arms and scared her all over again," I said.

Mick grunted. "She did the yelpin'. She knew what had happened," he said. "She was the first one I seen."

"First one you saw," I corrected.

Vennell stood up and glared at me. "What in hell is this—a class in grammar?" he muttered.

I looked serious. "You having the boat searched?" I questioned.

He nodded, frowning. "Of course. But no one seems to have seen the fellow, after Carla. She didn't see much more than I did. He was medium in size. She says his eyes 'burned.' "

"Sure," I replied. "She'd say that."

Vennell said sharply: "Well, what's to be done?"

I shrugged. "Mick had better bunk in here with you," I said. "We'll just say he's big and would like to get a crack at this guy. No use trying to hide the fact that he's in here. His feet are too big."

Mick O'Rourke muttered something I didn't catch. Vennell said:

"That fellow might have killed me while I was sleeping. And he could have got on deck, got rid of that black stuff—"

I interrupted. "He was medium-sized, eh?"

Vennell said. "About your build—but the light was bad, and he wore the robe loosely."

I looked at Vennell's right hand, half-hidden in his right pajama pocket. I said:

"What have you got there?"

Vennell narrowed his eyes. "The gun," he said. "The one that was on the table."

I nodded. "Why didn't you shoot at him?" I asked slowly. "Before he went out?"

Vennell grunted. "He was gone before I could reach for the gun. The door slammed. When I got outside, there were screams, and I was afraid of hitting someone. Then I heard Mick's voice, questioning Carla."

I nodded. Don Rayne and Cy Dana were outside; Vennell told them to come in. They said nothing had been seen of the intruder.

Vennell sat down and frowned at the floor. I said to Mick:

"You'd better come back and get fixed to spend the rest of the night in here. All right with you, Eric?"

Vennell nodded. Don Rayne said: "We'll stick until you get back, O'Rourke. But what's the reason for all this—"

He broke off, looking from Mick to me. I smiled a little.

"You got those diamonds in here, Eric?" I said, giving him a lead.

He almost missed it; his eyes staring into mine stupidly. Then he said:

"Hell, no. But I've got the fakes in here."

I said: "Someone doesn't know they're fakes, maybe. Come on, Mick—you need something to cover up that pajama color."

We went outside. As we neared Suite B, Bryce came along. I spoke to him softly.

"Carla better now?"

He nodded. "Shock mostly. Bruises on her arms, though. Just starting to show."

I said: "How about her throat?"

Bryce shook his head, smiling a little. His eyes were very blue.

"I'm afraid she imagined more than really happened. It's often the case. No finger marks on her throat, or bumps on her head. And the throat skin is quite delicate."

I nodded. "That's the Hollywood complex," I said. "It works the same way with salaries on the lot. A little bit goes a long way."

The doctor nodded and moved on. We went into Suite B and I locked the door behind us. Mick lighted a cigarette and grinned at me.

"Nice party, ain't it?" he said. "Who's the biggest liar of the lot?"

I frowned. "Don't yell," I said. "And stick in character. You haven't pulled a fast one in a long time. Use the one about liking to study Greek classics in the Latin countries because of—''

He swore. ''I can't remember it,'' he said. ''To hell with it. This other is better.''

I sat in a chair and said softly: ''Something's up, Mick. Sure as the devil. Clara wasn't choked—and her head wasn't banged against the corridor wall. Vennell thinks his life is in danger, yet when he sees a masked man coming into a cabin whose door has been locked, he calls out first and *then* reaches for his gun. After that he doesn't seem to have done much.''

Mick said grimly: ''That Sard frail did the rest. She was acting all over the corridor when I reached her. She had her arms over her face, and I pulled them down to look at her. I thought maybe she'd been slugged in the eye.''

I said: ''We'll try the one about the robber thinking Vennell had a lot of diamonds in his suite. It may fool some of the lot.''

Mick nodded. ''There's something funny,'' he said.

I reached into a pocket of my flannels and took out the folded yellow slip. Mick said:

''What you got?''

He came over and I unfolded the paper. It was a radiogram form, with typewritten words. It was addressed to Vennell. I read aloud: ''Boys using the tarpaulin. Three two one. Looks like a street sweeping on the gem. Western Branch. Casey.''

There was no date line on the radiogram. Mick muttered the words the second time. I said:

''You'd better get a robe, and hop over with Vennell. Don't get talking too much. I don't think anything more will happen tonight.''

The big fellow said: ''What about that thing?''

I shook my head. ''It may mean something,'' I said. ''And it may not.''

Mick frowned at me. ''Where'd you get it?'' he asked.

I groaned. "Found it," I said.

Mick whistled tonelessly. "You're having luck that way, ain't you?" he said.

I smiled. "Maybe *this* wasn't meant to be found," I said. "You get going—I've got some thinking to do."

Mick moved toward his bed. "If you need any help—" he started, but I cut in.

"I'll get in touch with you," I said. "So long, Mick."

It was an hour or so before things quieted down on the *Virgin*. I had a shot of Vennell's good Scotch and got to work on the radiogram. The *"Looks like a street sweeping on the gem"* came first. Someone figured it was a cleanup on Columbia, in the varsity race. I figured it that way, and that made the *"Three two one"* fairly easy. The odds were three to one. The *"Boys using the tarpaulin"* was a little more difficult. I got it suddenly, after another Scotch. The boys were covering up. Covering up money. California money.

I sat back in the wicker chair and felt very pleased with myself. Vennell was betting on Columbia to win the big race. He was getting odds of three to one, and someone using the fake name of Casey had radioed him that everything was all right in the betting end.

I said softly: "Columbia—the gem of the ocean."

Then I sang it. After that I started wondering about Sonia Vreedon. Had she dropped the radiogram? Why had Tim Burke stroked his way out to the yacht? Just a lovers' meeting? I didn't think so. It was a little too tough on Tim.

If Sonia *had* dropped the folded paper, where had *she* got it? Or perhaps Vennell had dropped it. That led me into a new line of thought. There was the business card I had picked up, in the smoke room. And now the suite affair, with both Vennell and Carla lying. Vennell because he had said the door slammed *first,* and when he got outside, there were screams. I'd heard the two screams first, distinctly; and *then* the door crash. And Carla because she had said she'd been choked and had her head banged against the corridor wall. But there were no bruises on her throat—just those of Mick's big fingers on her arms.

I thought: These people are amateurs, of course. But they're trying for something. And amateurs often improve rapidly.

The yacht bells struck five o'clock. I got into bed and listened to the distant, wailing whistle of a passenger train. Vennell was betting on Columbia, to win. California was the favorite. The odds were three to one. I had a sudden idea, got up, switched on one light, and got the dictionary from my luggage. It wasn't much of a book, but it was good enough for my tabloid column. Once in a while it gave me a new two-syllable word that could be understood in the subway. I looked for a three-syllable word this time. When I found it I read very softly:

"*Regatta*—a boat race or a series of races. Italian: *Regetta*—strife. *Re*—again. *Cattare*—get. *Capto*—catch. *Capio*—take."

I closed the book, got it back in a piece of luggage, switched off the light, and got into bed. The *Virgin* didn't seem to be rolling so much now. I closed my eyes and breathed softly into the darkness:

"A race. To get—to catch—to take. Strife."

I said "Sure" a couple of times, thinking of one thing or another sleepily. Hudson water lapped and swished against the *Virgin*. All sound became merged and unimportant. I dozed off.

•4•

REGATTA

Mick O'Rourke woke me by battering on the door. I let him in; he was grumbling. My watch showed that it was almost nine o'clock. I said:

"What's wrong with you?"

He told me that Eric Vennell had taken a long time getting asleep, and that after he'd got to sleep, he'd snored continuously. I went into the suite's shower, had one, and came out again. Mick was still grumbling. I shaved, and only cut myself once.

"What sort of a day is it?" I asked him.

Mick grunted: "Why don't you look out of the window? It's hot and clear. It's going to be hotter."

I nodded. "But not clearer," I told him. "The varsity race is always rowed in a lightning storm, a rough river, or in the darkness."

Mick said: "Why?"

I put powder on my face. "The officials don't believe in pampering the boys," I replied. "They only have to row four miles, and too many of them are able to sit up in their rigs at the finish. The officials don't like to see 'em sitting up."

Mick said: "You're kidding me."

I nodded. "That's true," I replied. "But I'll cut it out, now that you've discovered it."

The big fellow went into the shower room and started to sing, I said:

"It's too early for that—I haven't had breakfast, and it's tough. Just splash around."

He came out stripped and gave me a scare. Aside from a flock of bullet scars around his belly, he was something at once awe-inspiring and beautiful.

"Vennell's acting pretty worried this morning," he said. "He seems to think something's going to happen today."

I thought of the radio. "It is," I said grimly. "Maybe he's afraid it won't be the right thing."

Mick blinked at me. "I ran into that Sard moll," he said after a little pause. "I told her I was sorry about pinching her arms."

I whistled. "You're getting highbrow, Mick," I said. "What did she do when you told her that?"

He grinned. "She said: 'Like hell you are!' " he replied.

I shook my head sadly. "There's too damn much cursing on this boat," I said slowly. "No respect for her name."

Mick thought that was funny. He sat down and roared with laughter. I dressed in white, and felt sort of snappy. Mick looked me over and said in a thin voice:

"Lily—lily of the valley!"

I blew him a kiss. "You get dressed and stick close to Vennell," I said. "You don't take this business seriously enough. Didn't he give you five grand?"

The big fellow nodded. His face got serious.

"You get two of it, Al," he said. "Ths ain't such a bad racket, at that."

I said quietly: "Just the same, don't get too careless. Things are happening that seem funny, but they may not be. Vennell's keen—he's taken chances for his money.

He's a big-time gambler. He's not handing five grand out for nothing."

Mick's eyes were hard; his even teeth were pressed together. He separated them.

"Don't I know that!" he breathed.

He dressed, and remembered the radio. When he asked me the question, I said very softly:

"I don't know, but it looks as though Vennell is putting a lot of money on one of the crews. The radio might have told him that it was covered—at odds of three to one."

Mick stopped trying to tie a bow around his neck and stared at me.

"Which crew is he betting on?" he asked.

I grinned. "Columbia," I replied. "But if you lay the five grand the same way—you're crazy."

Mick said: "How much do you figure Vennell's betting?"

"Plenty," I replied. "He never bets the other way."

Mick started whistling and thinking. I knew he was thinking, because there were little wrinkles at the corners of his eyes. I said:

"I'm going to have breakfast on deck—would you care to join me?"

He grinned and bowed. *"Avec plaisir,"* he said, and reached for my hand.

I got it away from him. "Where'd you learn *that*?" I muttered.

He grinned with delight. "At Frenchy's speak, in Chicago," he said. "I fooled around there for a few weeks, on the lay for Little Louis."

I said: "Did Louis come in?"

He shook his head, still grinning. "He *started* in," he said. "But one of the Flaco mob got him in the alley."

I got a pack of cigarettes. "Tough," I said. "You learning bad French—and some other guy guns out Little Louis."

Mick O'Rourke made a sweeping gesture with his big right hand and started to work on the bow tie again.

"It's the breaks," he said. "Just the breaks."

I nodded. "if you don't have any luck with that bow, ring for Griggs," I suggested. "The race starts just before dark, maybe."

The big fellow chuckled. "I'll have it by dark," he came back. "What's that one about what I'm supposed to think of Italy?"

I groaned. "You found little youth there," I said. "The people, even the younger ones, seemed old. It was like expecting a child to be happy among monks, in a monastery."

Mick repeated it slowly. I said: "Pirandello said that."

The big fellow blinked at me. "No?" he muttered. "And Jackie Fields knocked him out in the fourth, last week!"

I covered my face with my palms and groaned. When I looked at Mick again, he was working on the tie.

"Pirandello's an Italian playwright," I said, "Not a pug."

Mick swore softly. "It's a good line, anyway," he replied.

I moved toward the door. "He'd be glad to know you liked it, Mick," I said.

The big fellow grinned. "Only these monks—they like their liquor, Al. Why *couldn't* a guy be happy among monks?"

I went out, slamming the door. Every once in a while Mick O'Rourke pulled one that was tough to answer.

2

At lunch Don Rayne told me that the Columbia crew was in fine shape. Cy Dana went to the California boathouse, and when he came back, he said the varsity-shell boys were in fine shape. He said that the Navy crew looked great, and that Dartmouth and Penn were fit.

Syracuse had a husky crew, and the other shell outfits looked perfect.

"Strange," I told the two of them. "I sort of figured the boys would be in the shells with broken arms and legs, fractured skulls—"

Cy Dana shook his head. "Those things might happen on *this* craft," he said. "But the crews are in swell shape."

I said: "They'll all win, eh?"

Vennell came over to the table at which we were eating, on deck. He frowned at me.

"The yacht's been searched thoroughly," he said. "We haven't found a thing."

He shook his head. The color of his skin wasn't so good and his eyes looked tired. Cy Dana spoke.

"I hate to suggest it, but it looks to me as though one of the crew was after what he thought were real diamonds. He knew you had the stones. He got clear, chucked that face mask and black robe overboard. No one was the wiser."

Vennell said: "It isn't a large crew, and Captain Latham has confidence in all the men."

I nodded. "Then there are the others—the guests."

Cy nodded, grinning at me. "I believe Miss Sard has said that the masked one was about your build, Al," he said.

Vennell swore. He shrugged his shoulders, looked from the awninged deck toward other craft near what was to be the finish line. The *Virgin* had a fine position, not far from the shadow of the new bridge.

"Going to be hot—and calm," he said. "Any of you boys betting?"

Cy Dana said that he had a hundred on California. I looked at Vennell curiously.

"How much have you got up, the same way, Eric?" I asked.

He smiled. "The Golden Bears look right to me," he said. "I'm taking it easy though—about fifty thousand, spread around the country."

Don Rayne whistled softly. "You don't fool," he said, and then looked silly.

Cy grunted. "I'll suffer more if I lose my hundred," he said.

Vennell smiled again. "We'll both clean up, Cy," he said. "But you fellows are paper boys; if you use the fact that I'm betting on California, don't spread it all over."

I turned away and lighted a cigarette. Vennell was saying something now. He was telling us that we could print his bet on California. He rather *wanted* us to print it. That opened up a new idea. I could see a reason for him getting Cy and me aboard. He was betting on Columbia, but he wanted us to record the fact that he had bet on California.

He looked at me as I turned around, with my cigarette lighted.

"Maybe I've got a few dollars more than fifty thousand—on the big race," he said in a peculiar tone. "I'm sure pulling for California."

He moved away, taking a pair of day-glasses from the case hanging about his neck. Cy looked at me and winked.

"He's got big money on the Bears," he said.

Don Rayne nodded. "A hundred thousand, at least."

I smiled. "It's a cinch," I said. "California by three lengths. If you've got money—you can make it."

I went away from the table and along the port rail. The river was filling up with large and small craft—flags streamed colorfully. It was around one o'clock—the sky was clear and the day was very hot. Launches kicked up white water as they chugged back and forth; there was a steady stream of traffic on the new bridge.

The figure of Sonia Vreedon was at the rail ahead of me. Her slender body was leaning on it; she was staring toward the California boathouse. I followed her gaze; there were signs of activity—the freshman race would start in a few hours and California had a crew entered.

She didn't hear me come up close. I said softly:

"Think Tim's getting nervous yet?"

Her body jerked just a little, then she controlled her feelings. She faced me with a faint smile. I liked her eyes and lips, and the way she talked. There was no fooling about her. She was keen.

"Probably," she said. "Wouldn't *you* be getting nervous?"

I said: "Not if I'd had plenty of sleep the night before."

Light flickered in her eyes. Her body was tense; it relaxed as she spread arms along the rail and looked steadily at me.

"Well—the coach sees to that," she said. "Tim's had his sleep, all right."

I nodded and looked down at the water. "It's calm," I observed. "Not much danger of the shells flooding."

Her eyes watched mine closely. She said: "What do you make of last night's affair?"

I said: "Which one?"

It startled her. She took a swift breath—one hand came away from the rail. Then she looked puzzled. I liked the way she did it; she was putting up a fight.

"The only one I know about," she replied. "The man breaking into Eric's suite."

I smiled. "He has a nice collection of diamonds," I said. "Perhaps one of the crew—"

She frowned. "Don't be foolish," she interrupted.

I smiled at her. "Where were you during all the excitement? Sleeping?"

She shook her head. "Aft, down below," she said quietly. "Close to the water, just watching the river."

I liked that, too. It prevented her from being caught in a lot of little traps.

"That so?" I said. "You didn't hear anybody go overboard, did you?"

Again there was the flickering in her cool eyes. She raised browned fingers and touched her banded hair.

"Just wave splashes—and the screams, of course."

She smiled enigmatically. I nodded.

"Carla's so temperamental," I said. "But then—I suppose she was frightened."

Sonia Vreedon half closed her eyes. "Why was she in the corridor?" she asked.

I grinned. "Being a man—I've been afraid to ask her," I said.

Sonia stopped smiling. "*That* isn't the reason she was there," she said. "All the cabins are extremely well appointed."

I looked serious. "Perhaps she was going into the library for a book," I suggested.

Sonia just looked at me. "Or," I said, "perhaps she, too, was going aft to listen to wave splashes."

The daughter of the criminal lawyer watched the smoke curl upward from my cigarette.

"You don't believe that *I* was doing that," she said firmly.

I looked hurt. "Why shouldn't I?" I said. "A lot of humans were restless last night. I was on deck myself."

Fear showed in her eyes, then went away. "You don't believe that *I* was doing that," she said.

"May I have one of your cigarettes?"

I gave her one, lighted it. I said: "Well—the fellow didn't get anything, anyway."

She looked toward Highlands and said: "How's Eric betting, do you know?"

I nodded. "California," I said. "Quite a bit, too."

She looked suddenly frightened. Her body was tense again. She said:

"Are you sure?"

I shrugged. "He just told a few of us that he was," I said. "Why?"

She waited for several seconds, then smiled a little.

"He's had bad luck lately, and it doesn't seem like such a good hunch," she said.

That was silly, and she knew that I knew it was silly.

I thought of the radiogram, and said in a casual voice: "Eric generally knows what he's doing—the California shell looks best on paper."

She smiled cheerfully. "Wouldn't it be nice if the race could be rowed on paper, instead of the Hudson?" she said.

"It wouldn't be so much fun to watch," I said. "California has the outside lane—she should finish within a hundred yards of the *Virgin*. And Columbia is only two lanes away from her. We'll have a nice view, even if the boys do have rougher going."

She nodded. "Babe Harron will stroke them to a win," she said firmly. "He's got to!"

There was a lot of feeling in the last three words. I kept my eyes half-closed on Sonia's. I nodded.

"The saying is that when the Babe pulls an oar, they all pull with him," I said. "And I guess he wants to pull one today—his last race."

Her eyes closed; her back was against the rail, arms spread along it. She smiled with her fine lips.

I said: "You haven't seen Tim Burke in several weeks, have you? Couldn't you get a peep at him, at the boathouse?"

She shook her head. "Coach is pretty stiff," she replied. "Coach runs crew, you know—there isn't much fooling."

I nodded sympathetically. "You might have tried to sneak it," I said. "Last night, say."

She opened her eyes and they met mine squarely. Her voice was very low and very steady.

"I wouldn't," she said. "Why should I?"

"I don't know," I replied. "Only they say love is swell."

She smiled at me. "And a hard-boiled columnist believes what they say?" she asked.

I nodded. "And what he sees," I said very slowly.

She straightened and looked suddenly down the deck, aft. Rita Velda called in her thin voice:

"Come on, Sonia—we're toasting the California freshman!"

Sonia looked at me. "You'll pardon me?" she said.

I smiled. "I'll do better than that," I said. "I'll toast with you."

We went back toward the group under the awning aft. A Navy destroyer hissed through the water, close to the *Virgin*. Most of the crowd had come on deck; Carla Sard looked pallid and very beautiful. Sport clothes helped Rita. The stewards were working over drinks. Rita said:

"A pretty scene—but the water's so gray. It isn't like Naples, the Cote d'Azur—or the Lido."

Mick O'Rourke pulled a deck chair near a table for Sonia. He said huskily:

"That's right—it ain't."

Rita faced him, amusement in her eyes. She said:

"You agree with me, Mr. O'Rourke?"

He shrugged. "The Continent—it's too old. The people—they're old. Me, I don't like it. It's like asking a brat to stick around these monks, in a monastery."

The scar on his right cheek twisted as he said it. The girl with the blondish hair and the baby-blue eyes, who had stood beside Torry Jones when our launch had come alongside the *Virgin,* stared at the big fellow. Her name was Wilson or Tilson, and she did sketches of some sort.

"Well, Well!" she said.

Mick looked at her and smiled apologetically.

"Pirandello said it first," he explained.

Cy Dana sighed heavily. He looked at me and shook his head.

"And Al read it next," he muttered softly.

I frowned at him and passed a drink to Sonia. It was orange juice and something, in a tall, green glass. Carla looked narrowly at Mick. Rita took a short pencil from a pocket and scribbled on a small piece of paper.

Carla said: "Look out, Al—Rita's stealing the stuff you want for that book."

Mick grinned at Rita. "Shall I throw her overboard?" he asked grimly.

Carla stood up and waved her arms. "You come near me and I'll kill you!" she said dramatically. "You—you louse!"

Mick turned and winked at me. "Say it isn't so, Al," he said in a pleading tone. "Say I'm not a louse!"

I grinned and looked at Vennell. His eyes were narrowed on Sonia's. She was looking toward the California boathouse, her face set. Rita said icily:

"It's one of the most remarkable yacht affairs I've ever attended. Does the ship burn crude oil?"

A gentleman with white hair and a gentle face rose from a chair near the starboard rail, removed glasses from his eyes, and bowed gracefully to Rita.

"Well said!" he congratulated. "One cannot help but feel it *does* burn crude oil."

He replaced his glasses and seated himself. Mick stared at him, then at me. He got ready to say something, but I shook my head. Sonia didn't appear to have heard anything that had been said. Vennell was still watching her. Rita raised her green glass.

"Here's to—all the crews that race!" she said.

"And more particularly to California," Cy Dana said cheerfully.

Eric Vennell lifted his glass and smiled with his eyes half-closed on those of Sonia Vreedon.

"To the *winning* crew!" he said. "To the Golden Bears!"

3

The sun was getting low when the California varsity shell was dropped into the water, and the crew got aboard. The observation train moved slowly away from the track spot opposite the finish line, chugging back toward the starting point. Dartmouth's shell was pulling very slowly northward; other shells were ahead of her. The banks on both sides of the river were crowded with people in white; there was cheering as the Golden Bear shell stroked slowly away from the boathouse.

The siren of the *Virgin* wailed again and again; from the deck we could see Ed Dale, the diminutive coxswain, and the face and broad shoulders of Babe Harron. Sonia had her day-glasses raised; I was watching Tim Burke, saw him raise a hand and wave back.

Overhead two pontooned planes roared; there were others northward, over the starting line. Two destroyers were keeping the course clear. From the distance there was a rumbling sound; Don Rayne, standing beside me, swore.

"Storm," he breathed. "Always something—at the Poughkeepsie Regatta."

I looked to the northwest; there were dark clouds, not so far off. But the sky above was clear; there was hardly a breath of wind. The California boys were stroking very slowly and steadily up the river. Band music drifted from the east shore.

Mick came over to me. "There's a gal on board with a plump face and figger," he said. "She's cute, and I don't think we were introduced."

I nodded: "That's a break for her," I said.

He grinned. "You know her name?" he asked.

I shook my head. "There are five or six humans running around this yacht whose names I don't know," I said. "This is an informal party—go up and talk to her."

Mick looked relieved. "There's an idea," he said, and went away.

I walked up forward and saw Vennell coming toward me. He was nervous, and his eyes looked very bad. His fingers were opening and closing. He made a gesture and said:

"Nice show, Al—always is."

I nodded. I lowered my voice. "If you don't think Mick's sticking close enough, tell him so," I said.

Vennell frowned. "That's all right," he said. "And I wanted to thank you for thinking up that diamond story last night."

I smiled. Vennell said: "We'll get the start and reports until the shells are in sight—on the radio. They've got announcers all along. They should get off in fifteen or twenty minutes now."

I nodded. "That reminds me," I said. "I'd like to send a radiogram to my sheet."

Vennell's lips twitched a little. "Damn!" he breathed. "I'm sorry, Al—the sending set's gone bad. Carew has been working over it for two hours. Some fool thing. He may have it right by the time the race is over."

I lighted a cigarette. "How's the receiving set?" I asked.

He shook his head. "It may be aerial trouble," he said. "We haven't had a message since we left New York. It's tough."

He went along aft, and I stood for a few minutes and tried to think why he'd lied to me. Then I went on forward and ran into the captain.

"I want to send a radio," I told him. "Where's the spark shack?"

He looked sorry. "Too bad," he said. "But something went wrong just after we left New York. We can't get a message in or out."

I said: "Well, I can get ashore right after the race. Got to get something to the sheet—for tomorrow's column."

The captain nodded. I went on forward and watched the crowd along the Palisades on the west bank. They were milling round some, as usual. There had been an hour's wait between the first and second races—and more than an hour had passed after the second. It was growing a little dusky, and the thunder rumble was stronger and coming at more frequent intervals.

I muttered to myself: "They'd better—get things going."

When I went back aft, things were very quiet. The thunder roll came more loudly, but not so frequently. There was no cheering. Vennell was pacing back and forth; stewards were still making drinks and serving them. Mick was talking to the plump-faced girl, near a rail. I found an empty chair and sat in it. A steward brought me a drink. There was pretty much of an air of suppressed excitement. I watched Vennell and tried to figure what his reasons were for betting on Columbia. I was very sure he'd done just that.

The radio loudspeaker was making sound: some chap who kept informing his listeners that he was Carleton Tracy announced that all the crews but three were behind the starting line. He described the scene again and again and cracked bad jokes in between descriptions.

Vennell stopped pacing and said: "If the storm breaks before the finish—"

He checked himself. It was almost as though he had spoken aloud. Mick turned his head away from the girl with the plump face.

"Do they do it again tomorrow?" he asked. "If it rains?"

Vennell's body got rigid; his face grew red. He took steps toward Mick, pulled himself up short. He said in a fierce tone:

"Listen, you big—"

His arms had come up a little—they dropped to his sides. His voice died and his body relaxed. A slow smile spread across his face. He got out a handkerchief and tapped his forehead.

"I'm sorry, O'Rourke," he said in a low tone. "It's my nerves. Didn't mean anything."

He turned away. Mick looked at me with narrowed eyes. Vennell started to move forward; I watched Sonia Vreedon half rise, staring at the yacht owner's back. Then she dropped back in the chair again. Mick said slowly:

"That's all right—"

The radio announcer was saying that all the shells were lined up, that it was a beautiful sight—that it looked like a great chance for a start. The water was calm and there was no wind—

A cannon boomed sound from the distance. The radio announcer pitched his voice several octaves higher.

"They're off!" he was saying. "A pretty start. Can't say anything yet. Maybe Washington is out ahead some. Not very much. She seems to be stroked up a bit faster. Yes, she's pulling out. Dartmouth is sticking pretty close. California got away good, but it looks as though Columbia was left a bit. Doesn't matter much in a four-mile row. It's a beautiful sight, folks!"

I got out of my chair and went over near Cy Dana. He was making notes, but he looked up and grinned at me. Along with the announcer's voice there was the roar of plane engines, picked up by the mike he was using. Cy said:

"Vennell's pretty shaky, eh?"

I frowned. "You'd be, too—if a masked human got into your cabin—and then got clear again."

"Yeah," Cy said slowly. "I would—*if* a masked man got into my cabin and got clear again."

The loudspeaker cracked at intervals—there was more

thunder now, and it was louder. The sky was getting dark, but there was no wind. It was very hot. The captain came to Vennell's side and spoke. Vennell nodded, and the captain went away. Vennell said:

"The captain says we're due for a sharp storm. The yacht's shipshape, but you might have to move around while they get some of the awning stuff reefed. The stewards'll take care of the cabins—and we've plenty of anchorage room."

Sonia Vreedon was out of her deck chair; she, too, seemed very nervous. Cy Dana said to me:

"I know how Vennell feels—even my hundred buck bet makes me nervous."

The storm seemed to be holding off. At the first mile Washington, rowing in an inside lane, had a two-length lead. Dartmouth and Columbia were rowing on almost even terms. Navy and Syracuse were bunched with California, in a third group. Wisconsin and Cornell led Penn by a length. That was the way it looked to the announcer, who figured it would also be a race between the crews and the storm.

Vennell listened and said: "Dartmouth does like any green crew—rows herself out. California'll get up there."

At the second mile there were two changes in position. Columbia had pulled away from Dartmouth, and Navy was on even terms with the crew that was rowing its first race in a Poughkeepsie Regatta. California was four lengths behind the leader, Washington; and that crew still had a two-length lead.

I had another drink, and so did most of the others. Vennell smoked one cigarette after another and tried unsuccessfully to stay in one spot for more than ten seconds. Mick O'Rourke kept staring up the river and announcing that he couldn't see the boats. There was a little wind now, and the lightning crackled more through the loudspeaker.

At the third mile Columbia was within a half-length of the Huskies, and California was a length behind Columbia. Dartmouth was splashing and falling rapidly behind. Penn's light crew was falling back. Navy and Cornell were fighting it out for fourth place. Syracuse was in sixth, and Wisconsin was doing badly in seventh. The announcer at this point along the Hudson figured it was between Washington, Columbia and California. He thought the Golden Bears were hitting the best stroke—the cleanest. They were beautiful to watch.

Vennell was smiling. "The last mile!" he breathed. "We should see 'em pretty quick now. But that damn wind—"

The water was roughing up; the wind made shrilling sounds in the Virgin's rigging. It was getting pretty dark. We were all at the rail, staring up the river. But we stayed there awhile without seeing anything. And then the bomb at the railroad bridge sounded—and we picked up the outlines of three shells.

The water was growing steadily rougher. An announcer stated that the Dartmouth shell had flooded, and that launches were going to her. She was lengths in the rear. Most of us had glasses. But Vennell was the first to call out.

"California!" he shouted. "She's got a good length lead!"

I focused my glasses and nodded my head. California had a length lead, perhaps more. The oars were splashing less than those of the Columbia crew, which was in second place. The river water was very rough. Washington looked to be in third place by a very narrow margin. Navy was giving her a fight. The other shells were difficult to place.

At the half-mile California had what looked to be a three-length lead. The shell was being pulled strongly. Columbia was still in second place, and Navy was ahead of Washington. Thunder drowned the voice from the loudspeaker, but I caught the words: "—and it looks like California to win!"

The wind was blowing in gusts—crew members were reefing in the awnings above us. Vennell and Sonia Vreedon were side by side at the rail—Sonia was calling in a hard low voice:

"Come on California—keep *up* there!"

We could see the crews clearly now—the leaders. An announcer said that the Wisconsin shell was swamped, and that Syracuse seemed to be in difficulty. I kept my eyes on the California crew. Cy Dana, on my left, said above the shrill of the wind:

"Don Rayne was right—California by three—"

He checked himself. I'd seen the splash, too. It was near the stern of the California shell, near the spot at which the coxswain's small body moved back and forth as it beat out the stroke. That splash meant ragged work—someone was weakening!

Cy said hoarsely: "Good God, Al—it's Babe Harron—*his* oar—"

I stared through the glasses, and thought of Sonia Vreedon's words, last night: "Please, Tim—" I said sharply to Cy:

"It's Burke's oar, isn't it? Number Seven?"

But even as I said it, I knew I was wrong. And Cy's voice said grimly:

"Wrong side of the shell. It's Babe Harron, the stroke!"

Sonia's voice reached me, pitched high. She said:

"Eric—Eric—the Babe—there's something wrong!"

I wanted to look at Vennell, but I didn't. That splash in the water, the slow drag—the off timing—it fascinated me. Babe Harron, the veteran of the California crew, the one man they depended on—the stroke. And he was faltering!

I looked at the Columbia shell. She was coming up

fast. The finish line was less than three hundred yards distant now—and only two lengths separated California and Columbia. Navy was perhaps two lengths behind Columbia, on an inner lane. The fact that California and Columbia were rowing in outside lanes made it easy to see, to judge.

Harron was barely pulling, lifting his oar now. It seemed to me that he was twisting his head a little, holding it high. Ed Dale was trying to splash water on him—the whole crew was rowing raggedly. Columbia was within a length of the Golden Bears now, as the yacht whistles commenced to shriek!

The siren of the *Virgin* wailed; a sharp clap of thunder followed a lightning flash. The wind had died some—now it swept across the river. I kept my glasses on the California shell; watched the wood of the Columbia boat come into focus, saw how rapidly the second-place shell was gaining. Beside me Cy was swearing in a dull, monotonous voice. Whistles, thunder, radio announcing, and cheers were coming in bursts now.

A hundred yards from the finish Columbia was on even terms with the Golden Bears. Almost instantly she shot ahead. Navy was closing in now. I heard Carla Sard scream shrilly:

"It's Columbia—Columbia's race!"

I got my glasses on the California shell. The boys were pulling, but their stroke was ragged. Babe Harron was swaying in his slide rig; even as I watched him he suddenly collapsed, his head going toward Dale's body. Navy's shell was on even terms now. There was the roar of guns—whistles fought with thunder in sound.

I lowered my glasses, looked toward the finish line. Columbia was across, the winner. The Navy crew, hitting a fast beat, shot across in second place. Raggedly pulled, but still fighting, the California shell finished third.

I swung away from the rail in time to see Vennell

move forward along the deck. His fists were clenched at his sides—his body seemed to be shaking. Don Rayne was staring at me, eyes grim. For a second I faced Sonia Vreedon—she seemed stunned. There were tears in her eyes. I heard Cy Dana muttering:

"What do you know about—the Babe keeling over?"

Launches were rushing downstream to the shells that had crossed the finish line. I turned my back to the others, saw Eric Vennell's body vanish from sight, swaying, behind some superstructure. I moved after him, and as I moved, the first of the rain came. And with it a shrilling, tearing wind.

I called sharply: "Vennell—Eric!"

What I had to say I wasn't sure about. But I knew that Columbia had won, after California's stroke had collapsed. And I knew that Eric Vennell had won a tremendous sum of money, at odds of three to one. I knew that he had lied to me.

Rain beat down, and I had to fight wind along the deck. Vennell was nowhere in sight. I went below and looked for him there. No one seemed to have seen him after he had turned away from the rail. He had simply dropped out of sight.

4

We started an organized search after about twenty minutes. The storm lasted almost that long. Cy Dana had the captain lower the power launch, while we searched. After a half-hour we had found no trace of Vennell. Fifteen minutes later the launch came alongside, in water that was rough, but calming. Cy climbed the rope ladder, his face grim.

"Find Vennell?" he asked.

I told him we hadn't. He said no person in any craft near by had seen a man in the water. He said he'd gone to the California boathouse. He was soaked, and I went down to his cabin with him.

When we got inside, he closed the door. He smiled grimly at me.

"I fought my way inside, and I learned things, Al," he said. "You held back on me, but I won't do it with you. Babe Harron is dead."

I stared at him. "Dead?" I muttered. "You mean he collapsed and then—"

Cy stopped smiling. "He didn't collapse and then," he said. "*When* he collapsed, he *was* dead."

I said softly: "Bad heart—"

Cy nodded. "And the mark of a hypodermic syringe needle, between the shoulder blades," he said very slowly.

I stood motionless, and after a few seconds I reached for a cigarette, got it between my lips.

Cy said: "There's to be an autopsy—God knows where. Probably Poughkeepsie, perhaps Kingston. I talked with that crew doctor, Vollmer. He says it's murder."

I said: "Murder, eh?"

Cy nodded. "Harron *was* in perfect shape—nothing wrong with his heart. Murder—by poison injected through a hypodermic syringe."

I sat down and half closed my eyes. "And California lost," I said slowly.

Cy Dana spoke grimly. "And Columbia won," he said.

I looked at the cabin wall. "And Vennell has disappeared," I said in a half-whisper.

The sportswriter swore very quietly. There were footfalls beyond the cabin door, heavy ones. Mick O'Rourke's voice sounded.

I got up and opened the door. Mick was breathing heavily.

"What's wrong?" I asked.

Mick drew a deep breath. "I've got a hell of a toothache," he said. "What'll I do for it?"

Cy Dana turned his back and muttered to himself. I said:

"Take a water glass of Scotch. With Vennell gone you haven't got anything else to do."

I shut the door, and Mick's feet made a lot of sound and then less.

Cy Dana faced me, his eyes squinted. After a few seconds he said:

"I don't think that guy's half so funny as he acts. How much do *you* know that I *don't* know, Al?"

I thought of the scar across Mick O'Rourke's cheek, and I could see Dingo Bandelli slashing with the knife, and Mick's fists battering at him. I looked at the sports-writer and wondered how much of a lie I was telling.

"Not very much," I said.

•5•

RED SUNSET

MICK O'ROURKE'S broad shoulders caught my eyes, in the smoke room, as I moved along the corridor. It was past the hour for the gay dinner that was to have followed the varsity race, but with Babe Harron dead and Vennell missing from the yacht, I guessed dinner would be held up a bit.

Mick didn't hear me until I got right behind him. There was no one else in the room; the big fellow held a water glass in his left hand; it was half filled with yellowish liquid.

I said: "How's the toothache?"

He straightened a little, as though surprised, but I had a feeling he knew I'd reached the entrance to the smoke room. There was nothing the matter with Mick's ears.

"Not so hot," he said, and turned around.

My voice was a little grim, though I didn't want it to be that way.

"You certainly earned that five grand," I said.

The big fellow scowled. "I was watchin' the boats," he said. "There was a lot going on—in the river."

I nodded. "And there was a lot going on—on the *Virgin,*" I replied.

Mick frowned at me and tilted his glass. When he took it away from his lips again, he shook his head very slowly.

"I can't figure it, Al," he said. "Where do you suppose he got to?"

I groaned. "He got overboard," I said. "There was a lot of excitement, and everybody was watching the finish line. So the people in the other boats didn't see him hit water."

The big fellow grunted. "They'd see him swimming," he said.

I lighted a cigarette and looked down at Mick's big feet.

"What makes you think he swam?" I asked, after a little while.

Mick swore very softly. "You think he just went under—and didn't come up?" he breathed.

I said: "Why not?"

I started to put my cigarette pack away, but the big fellow grabbed for it. He got a cigarette loose and I struck a match. Mick inhaled.

"That means you think someone slugged him, Al," he said finally.

I shrugged. "He isn't aboard the *Virgin,*" I said. "And that makes me think he went overboard. Maybe he didn't come up from his dive."

Mick said: "He lost a lot of coin, Al. With California losing that way. Maybe he suicided."

I smiled a little. "*Did* he lose a lot of coin, Mick?" I asked.

The big fellow was getting sore. He half shut his dark eyes, and the scar across his right cheek twitched a little.

"Jees, Al—" he breathed grimly—"I don't get you."

I nodded. "You saw that crew man collapse—in the California shell?" I asked.

Mick nodded. "There was a guy did the same thing in the Columbia shell," he said. "But they splashed water on him and he sat up."

I said: "Well, they splashed water on Babe Harron, too. But it didn't do any good. Cy Dana just got back from the California boathouse. Harron's dead."

Mick O'Rourke looked surprised. He said:

"Jees—he's dead, eh?"

I nodded. "And he was the strongest man in the California shell, Mick. And he was in swell condition. And when he collapsed—that finished things. Columbia got the win, and Navy got in second. Babe Harron was dead when the other men pulled him across the line."

Mick said: "Yeah—bad heart, eh?"

I swore at him. I got my voice very low.

"Listen, big boy—" I said—"I don't like to see you being too dumb. Harron was murdered. A hypodermic needle got the stuff inside of him."

Mick whistled softly and kept his eyes widened on mine.

"What stuff?" he asked.

I shook my head. "There hasn't been an autopsy yet," I said patiently.

He lifted his glass and took another drink of the yellowish liquid. He shook his head from side to side. I watched him and waited.

"Say!" he said suddenly. "If this fellow Harron hadn't collapsed, California would have won!"

I drew a deep breath. I sang softly and grimly:

"I think—you're wonderful. . . ."

Mick didn't pay any attention to me. He was staring into space.

"And Vennell would have won a lot of coin, instead of losing it," he said.

I waited a few seconds. Then I got fingers around Mick's big wrist, part of the way. I said very softly and with a lot of feeling:

"Listen, Mick—I pulled you in on this deal. You don't have to be dumb with me. It's all right with the others—"

The big fellow made a short movement and got his wrist away from my fingers. He put his glass down on the table.

"Don't get hard that way, Al!" he said.

I smiled at him. I said quietly: "If I took you in to a Poughkeepsie dentist right now, he'd say you were just imagining things."

Mick narrowed his eyes and looked down at me with a faint smile playing around his thick lips. I said:

"You haven't got any toothache—and you didn't have any when you came down below while I was talking to Cy Dana."

Mick said: "No?"

I shook my head. "No. And you knew the stroke was dead—before I told you, just now."

He blinked at me. "You're going crazy, Al," he said. "How in hell would I know that guy Harron was dead?"

I said: "You heard Cy Dana tell me—down in the cabin."

The big fellow let his lower jaw sag a little. He said sadly:

"You're crazy, Al."

I nodded. "Then you tiptoed away and made a racket coming back, with your big feet," I said. "Then you handed the toothache line to us."

Mick grunted. "Yeah?" he said. "And what was the big idea of me doin' all this stuff?"

I touched cigarette ash with a nail, and the white stuff missed the tray on the table by an inch.

"I haven't had time to figure that out, Mick," I said. "What I'm trying to get across to you is that you can't work the dumb racket with me. It might go with the others. I'm not so sure of that."

The big fellow caught me by the shoulder and swung me around. He slitted his eyes.

"Go easy, Al," he gritted. "If you're bein' funny, just let me know."

I said: "Take your hands off me, Mick. Don't act up. You're in a tough spot right now."

He took his time, but after a few seconds he spread his big fingers and looked a little sheepish. Then he said:

"You know I don't sneak around, Al."

I smiled at him. "You know what I know," I replied. "That's the way I wanted it to be."

The big fellow frowned at me. He was silent for a little while. Then he said slowly:

"What do you mean—I'm in a tough spot right now, Al?"

I listened to the piping whistle of a small launch and heard a voice that sounded like Captain Latham's answer a hail. Mick said again:

"What do you mean, Al?"

I said: "I've got a hunch that it won't be long before the police come aboard the yacht. Latham's sent a boat ashore to report Vennell's disappearance. Babe Harron is dead. They may try to tie the things up."

The big fellow was frowning. "How does that put *me* in a tough spot?" he asked.

I said: "Be yourself, Mick. You're no member of the First Methodist Church. You may be recognized."

He grunted. "What of it?" he muttered. "I been recognized before, ain't I?"

There was something in that. But not enough to check my line of thought.

"This is a little different," I said. "Vennell is missing, and the stroke of the California crew is murdered. And you're aboard the *Virgin*. It might strike the police as being a little strange."

Mick swore. "He hired me as a bodyguard, didn't he?" he asked.

I said grimly: "And what a dud you turned out to be!"

The big fellow showed his white teeth, and his cheek scar stood out more clearly than usual.

"I don't follow you, Al," he said slowly.

I nodded, "And you didn't follow Vennell—not too closely," I replied.

Mick O'Rourke let his big arms swing at his sides. He smiled at me almost pleasantly. He said:

"You think I'm crossing you up, Al. You don't think I was tryin' to earn the five grand."

I made a clicking sound. "Mick," I told him, "you're a big guy, and you're tough. But it always seemed to me you were a pretty good guy, too. I don't want to see you get in trouble while you're aboard the *Virgin*."

The big fellow threw back his head and laughed. It made a lot of noise. I said:

"Shut up, you damn fool! What's happened isn't funny like that."

He shut up. Then suddenly he got his head lowered a little and hardened his eyes. He spoke very slowly and quietly.

"You—Al Connors—don't you be worrying about me. I don't like guys worrying about me—not even white guys like you!"

He nodded his head and chuckled harshly. Then he went past me and along the corridor. I waited a few minutes and tried to think things clear. It didn't work. I left the smoke room and started for the deck. When I got near the saloon aft, a voice called out:

"Mr. Connors!"

I stopped and turned around. Carla Sard came up close to me. She looked as though she had been crying.

"Has any trace of Eric—"

She checked herself, and there were tears in her eyes. I smiled at her.

"Not a trace of him," I said. "But it might be a joke of some kind."

She looked angry. "A joke?" she said. "Eric doesn't joke like this."

I said: "Are you well acquainted with him?"

She looked a little surprised. "I met him in California, six months ago," she said. "I knew him pretty well, out there."

I nodded. "In Hollywood?"

She shook her head. "We were on location, near San Francisco," she replied. "He was living there, in that city. He had the yacht there, in the Bay."

I didn't say anything. There were shouts from the deck. Carla said:

"I'm so afraid—I think he lost a great deal of money. He was so anxious for California to win. And when Babe Harron failed—"

She dabbed at her eyes with a tiny handkerchief. I said:

"What do you think happened to Eric?"

She let her eyes get wide. They were very beautiful eyes, with mascara helping out a lot. She said in a whisper:

"I think—he jumped overboard!"

I frowned. Someone on deck called out hoarsely:

"Take it easy—we won't have any paint left! Shove off there!"

Carla said: "How long would it be—before—before—"

I looked serious. "Not too long," I said. "But I don't think you're right. I don't think Vennell has drowned. So you needn't worry about the body coming up."

She kept dabbing at her eyes. I wanted to go out on deck, but something kept me beside her. I asked:

"Where's Torry and Don Rayne?"

She shook her head. "I don't know where anybody is—I've been in my cabin. It's terrible—"

I said: "It'll be all right."

I went out on the deck, leaving her dabbing her eyes

with the damp handkerchief. Everything was pretty wet outside, but the clouds had broken in the west. There was a strange red light in the sky, faint, but reflected. Lights flickered along both shores. It was dark except for the red color. It was different from any sunset I'd seen before.

Captain Latham stood near the rail; I went over to him. Some of the crew were on deck. The yacht's launch was fifty feet or so from the *Virgin*, bobbing about in the water that was still a little rough. There was another launch close to the yacht, and a tall, thin man was coming up the dropped ladder. He wore a slicker and a soft hat, and he took his time in the climb.

I said to the captain: "Who's this?"

He looked at me as though he had never seen me before.

"The police," he said. "I sent for 'em."

Latham was a man of about forty-five. He was short and brown-faced, with gray hair. He had hard, gray eyes and a mouth that turned down at the corners. His lips were very thin, and they had a little color in them.

I looked toward the *Virgin*'s launch and saw that two of the crew were in it. Then the man coming up the ladder reached the deck. He had a hatchet-like face and deep-set, greenish eyes. Gray-green. He shoved his soft hat back a little and looked sharply at me. Latham said:

"I'm the captain—I sent for the police."

The thin one nodded. "I'm Risdon," he said. "I work in plain clothes, out of Poughkeepsie. What's wrong?"

He had a rasping voice, and he spoke like a businessman of major importance. Latham said:

"Eric Vennell, the owner of this yacht, has disappeared."

Risdon made a sniffling noise. "What of that?" he snapped.

Latham said: "It was just after the finish of the race,

and the storm had just broken. We searched the yacht thoroughly. He isn't aboard."

Risdon looked at me. "You one of the guests?" he asked.

I nodded. Latham said, with a touch of grimness in his voice:

"From what I can find out—Mr. Connors was the last person to see Mr. Vennell."

I didn't like the captain's tone. He suddenly assumed importance to me. After all, he was Vennell's captain. And the yacht had been in San Francisco Bay, six months ago. That seemed to be important, too, though I couldn't figure just why.

Risdon looked at me steadily and said: "Well, what do you think happened to this man Vennell?"

I shook my head. "I haven't the slightest idea," I said simply.

Risdon frowned at me. He looked at Latham and frowned at him. I watched a launch leave the California boathouse dock and head straight for the anchorage spot of the *Virgin*. Risdon said:

"Was Vennell sober?"

I nodded. "He seemed very sober," I stated.

Risdon said: "Well—the storm had wind. Maybe he went overboard."

Captain Latham said: "Vennell was a strong man, and he's been aboard this craft when she's been in a lot tougher storms than this one. He's a strong swimmer. If he went overboard, it wouldn't bother him any."

Risdon said: "It would if he hit his head on something—as he went over."

The captain nodded. "Or it would if someone hit him on the head, *before* he went over!" he said grimly.

Risdon't lean body stiffened a little. He whistled softly.

"It's like that, eh?" he said.

Latham shrugged. "Let's go to my quarters," he said. "I've got some things to tell you."

Risdon looked at me. "You saw him last," he said slowly. "Don't go ashore Mr.—"

I said: "—Connors. I'll stick aboard, Mr.—"

He smiled with his lips. He said:

"—Risdon."

I nodded. Latham looked somewhere beyond me and spoke softly.

"A few things have happened aboard the *Virgin*, Risdon. I think you should know abut them."

Risdon said: "Sure, that's what I get paid for."

Latham moved away from the rail, and the detective turned a little and started to follow him. He stopped and said suddenly:

"What the—"

I looked toward the spot on which Risdon's eyes were focused. Mick O'Rourke had come on deck; he was moving aft and looking toward the Jersey shore. The red sunset put light on his big body; his right hand was clenched and swinging a little. His jaw was set and he looked tough. The scar stood out clearly.

Latham turned and said to Risdon: "That's one of the things I want to talk to you about."

The detective swore. He followed the captain, but he didn't look at him. He turned his head as though looking at the river. His body moved toward Mick's. When they collided, he reached out hands and touched Mick's arms. Mick did about the same thing. They both smiled and apologized.

Risdon's face was pretty close to the big fellow's, and I got the idea that the plainclothes dick wasn't missing much. They untangled and Risdon went along behind the captain. Mick came up to me, but he wasn't smiling.

"Where'd that dick come from?" he asked softly.

I said: "How'd you guess he was a detective?"

Mick swore. "He gave me the close eye," he said. "And he pawed me a little. What's up?"

I watched the launch coming out from the California boathouse. I thought of the business card I'd found, and the radiogram. I thought of a few other things.

Mick O'Rourke said grimly: "We're going to get asked questions, eh?"

I smiled. "Well, you've got the answers for 'em, haven't you, Mick?"

He narrowed his fine eyes and nodded his head very slowly. There was a peculiar tone to his voice.

"If I haven't—maybe I can work 'em up as I need 'em, Al," he replied.

I said: "It's a good theory."

Mick grunted. A slow smile spread over his big, battered face. He looked out over the water and said in an almost gentle voice:

"That red makes the water pretty, Al. Jees—but that's nice!"

I said: "Always the æsthete, Mick!"

He looked very wise. "That's me, Al," he returned. "I gotta yen for red."

"It's a nice color—against white," I said grimly.

He nodded and smiled pleasantly. "Yeah," he said. "If the guy's wearing that sort of a shirt."

2

We were standing and seated, in the main saloon of the yacht—the whole crowd of us. None of the crew were present. There was talk, but it was low and not particularly inspired. After a little while Captain Latham came in, followed by Risdon. The captain said, his face serious:

"Risdon here is from the Poughkeepsie police force. We've been trying to get at something. He's got something to say."

There was a lot of silence as Risdon moved his lean

body over near the grand piano and smiled round the saloon. He spoke slowly and cheerfully, in his rasping voice.

"I just don't want anyone to leave the yacht for a while," he said. "And if any of you know anything about Mr. Vennell that you think I should know—I'd be mighty glad to listen."

He looked round the group, his greenish eyes holding a questioning expression. I watched Sonia Vreedon; she was relaxed in her chair, watching the detective with her gray eyes narrowed. Torry Jones, who stood with his back against a side wall of the room, said loudly:

"Well, I guess we all know that *something* strange was going on. Someone broke into Vennell's cabin."

Risdon nodded. "So Captain Latham tells me," he said. "What was the motive, do you know?"

Jones shrugged. "Something was said about Vennell having some fake diamonds with him," he said.

Risdon nodded again. "But you don't think much of that idea, eh?" he asked.

Torry shrugged again. "It seems a little thick to me," he said, and took his eyes away from Risdon, looking at me.

I yawned. Cy Dana, sitting near Carla Sard and the blonde whose name I kept forgetting, spoke in a steady voice:

"I've got a story to file—to get to my paper, Risdon. I've got to get ashore."

I chuckled. Cy Dana stood up and frowned at me. I said:

"That's so—I've got one to get to New York, too. I almost forgot it."

Cy Dana muttered something I didn't catch. Risdon kept nodding his head. Finally he stopped nodding it.

"You two write your stuff, don't you?" he asked.

I grinned. "I write mine," I replied. "I don't know who writes Dana's."

Risdon's face got hard. "You seem pretty cheerful, Mr.—"

"—Connors," I said, and stopped smiling. "Not too cheerful, Mr.—"

He said grimly: "Well, write what you want. I'll see that it gets over the wire. But stay on the yacht."

I got up and said: "That's pretty stiff, Risdon. What's the charge? What's keeping us on the yacht?"

He said: "Suspicion of murder's the charge—and *I'm* keeping you on the yacht."

Carla Sard said: "But, Mr. Risdon—who would want to murder Eric Vennell?"

She put a lot of innocence in her words. Risdon was getting sore; it showed in his eyes and around his mouth.

"Where were *you*—when Vennell disappeared?" he snapped at her.

Carla let out a little scream. Mick O'Rourke, who had picked out the darkest spot in the saloon for his resting place, said huskily:

"Come to think of it, Watson—I don't recall seein' Carla at just about the time Vennell disappeared."

Torry Jones swung his body a little and said viciously:

"You're a damn liar, O'Rourke—she was at the rail, right beside you!"

Mick said in a surprised tone: "Was she? Well, Well!"

Carla got up and faced the big fellow. She said in a half-hysterical voice:

"I was—I was! You know that! You're just trying to ruin my career! If there's publicity—"

Risdon said sharply: "All right, all right! Don't let's get excited. I'll be out here for a while, and there's plenty of time."

Carla sat down, talking to herself. The blonde went over close to her and looked as though she were sympathizing. Torry said:

"You'd better talk to O'Rourke, Risdon. And Al Connors, too. He brought that big guy aboard, and none of us know why."

Risdon said slowly: "O'Rourke, eh?"

Torry nodded. "He attacked me," he said grimly. "He threw me overboard, last night."

Mick said tonelessly: "Let me kiss your hand, madame—"

Torry Jones snapped: "Listen, O'Rourke—"

Risdon said: "Cut it out—cut it out!"

He took a slip of paper from his pocket, and a stubby pencil. He made some scratches. Mick said to me:

"It looks like they've got me, Al. Didn't I chuck Jones overboard?"

I said: "You shouldn't have done it, Mick. But you always were impetuous."

Mick sighed. "It's my nerves," he muttered.

Captain Latham said in a hard voice: "It seems to me that Mr. Vennell surrounded himself with people having a strange sense of humor."

Risdon nodded his head. Don Rayne spoke very quietly.

"You use the past tense, Captain?"

The captain shrugged. I looked at Risdon.

"How can you hold us on the yacht, on suspicion of murder complicity, when you haven't any proof that Vennell has been murdered? Disappearance isn't murder."

The Poughkeepsie detective said:

"Vennell's life has been threatened. He has disappeared. He was afraid of death. That's enough for me."

Cy Dana looked at me. "He hasn't any authority on board the *Virgin*, has he, Al?" he asked.

I shrugged. "God knows," I said. "I suppose not. But, then, he could make things disagreeable."

Captain Latham said: "Well, *I* have authority on board the *Virgin*. My owner has disappeared. I order you folks to remain on the ship. The crew is remaining, also."

Risdon kept his eyes on mine. He spoke very quietly.

"I'd stay aboard if I were you, Connors," he said.

I nodded. "Perhaps you would," I agreed.

Sonia Vreedon spoke for the first time. Her voice was steady, cool.

"Can you tell us about Babe Harron? Has anything been learned about the manner—of his death?"

Risdon said slowly: "Two doctors believe he was drugged to death. Poisoned. I believe the police are trying to communicate with his father, who is in New York. They wish permission for an immediate autopsy."

There was silence. I looked at Risdon and decided he was pretty intelligent for a Poughkeepsie plainclothesman. Not that I knew anything about the detectives of that town; it was just a feeling I had. Risdon said:

"You see, I am perfectly frank with you people. No doubt some of you knew Harron."

No one said that they knew Babe Harron. I thought Risdon's voice was a little grim.

"Perhaps I'm mistaken, then."

He looked at me and said quietly: "I'm going to use the captain's quarters for my questioning. I think I'd like to talk with Mr. Torry Jones first."

He smiled a little, letting his eyes move over the bunch of us. Torry said:

"That suits me, Risdon," and moved toward the saloon door leading to the deck.

Mick O'Rourke looked at me and said in a voice that could be heard all over the room:

"Where were you on the night of the seventeenth, Connors? On the night of the twentieth? What—you *won't* answer? You won't, eh? Oh. yes you—"

He kicked wood of the wall and uttered a long-drawn groan. He said:

"Well—will you talk *now*?"

Carla Sard stood up and faced Mick. She said in a furious tone:

"You fool! Eric Vennell is dead—Babe Harron has been murdered. And yet you—"

She broke off. Torry Jones went over close to her and said quietly:

"Don't let him annoy you, Carla. He's just a roughneck without any decent instincts."

Risdon looked at Mick and nodded his head. He spoke quietly.

"My methods may not be like the ones you're accustomed to, Mr. O'Rourke."

The big fellow replied: "One way or the other—it's all the same to me. The only thing you'll get from me will be the truth."

Torry made a strange sound. I said:

"Well—how about dinner?"

Carla faced me and started to act again. She waved her arms around, but she waved them with considerable grace.

"You can talk of eating!" she raged. "You can even *think* of eating—"

I said: "Be yourself, Carla. I can do better than talking or thinking about it. I can eat."

She said dramatically: "With poor Eric—"

Mick said slowly: "I hope the chef has prepared spinach. I like spinach—"

Captain Latham said grimly: "Dinner will be served as usual."

Mick grunted. "Like hell it will," he said. "It's late already."

Carla said: "Oh," two or three times, and went from the saloon. Torry Jones followed her. Captain Latham and some of the others followed her. Risdon stood just inside the door that led to the deck and kept his greenish eyes narrowed on Mick. Finally, he said:

"Have you ever been on stage, Mr. O'Rourke?"

Mick looked at me, then at Risdon. He nodded his big head.

"I worked as a stooge for Phil Baker, out west," he said cheerfully.

Risdon nodded. "It's pleasant work," he said almost casually.

Mick smiled. "It keeps you up late, and the night air was bad for my chest. I had to quit."

Risdon smiled. "But you got the knack of acting," he said pleasantly. "That helps."

He went outside. Mick went over to a divan and sat down. He whistled tunelessly. Cy Dana came over and said:

"Like hell you worked as a stooge for Phil Baker!"

Mick shrugged. "Out west," he repeated.

I looked around. Sonia Vreedon was leaving the saloon. That left only Cy, Mick, and me. I said:

"Take it easy, Mick—this fellow Risdon isn't so dumb. And remember, Harron's dead."

Cy Dana spoke grimly: "If he was killed by a drug injection, that was sweet timing. Another sixty seconds and California would have been over the line—the winning shell."

I said: "It might not have been figured just that way. It almost failed to work, that's all."

The door shut behind the figure of Sonia Vreedon. I said to Mick:

"I don't think Vennell's dead."

Cy Dana was watching me narrowly. He didn't speak. There was a little smile on his lips. Mick O'Rourke drew a deep breath.

"In the Case of Raepner versus Lane, it was the contention of the State of Delaware, based on the transcript of the Case of the State of Montana against Wappinger, that the corpse is necessary proof—"

Cy Dana said grimly: "Well, the stroke is dead. Vollmer is the crew doctor, and he doesn't talk like a fool. He says it's murder."

I said softly: "Babe Harron's dead. Vennell has disappeared. Latham sent for the police, and unless I'm figuring all wrong, the copper that came aboard has brains. He's going to learn a lot of strange things."

Cy said: "Sure, Al. But I can't give him much."

I said: "I can't give him much."

We both looked at the big fellow. Mick reached for his cigarette pack.

"*I* can't give him anything but love," he said very grimly.

·6·

LITTLE WHITE LIES

SONIA VREEDON stood near the rail, aft, and looked toward the Jersey shore. I whistled a little as I approached. There was no one else aft, and it was pretty dark. Only a few stars showed through breaks in the clouds. At intervals thunder rumbled distantly.

Sonia heard me whistle and turned. She leaned against the rail with her arms spread along it. I had a funny feeling inside of me when I looked at her.

I said: "Has Risdon talked with you yet?"

She shook her head. Her gray eyes were on mine; her complexion was smooth and perfect. She was breathing a little quickly.

"Has he talked to you?" she asked.

I said that he hadn't. She said that she thought Don Rayne was inside the captain's quarters now, and that the detective seemed to be talking with the yacht guests one at a time.

I said: "That makes it easier—for him. If any of us make mistakes, he can check up. We don't know what the other fellow said."

She looked a little puzzled. ''Why should any of us make mistakes?'' she asked.

I said: ''Sonia—there might be a reason.''

A little color got into her cheeks. I smiled into her eyes.

''I can go back to the Miss Vreedon if you want me to,'' I said.

She shook her head. ''No, don't,'' she said. ''Be honest with me, will you, Al?''

I frowned a little. ''If it doesn't hurt too much,'' I agreed.

''Hurt you—or someone else?'' she asked.

I said: ''Me—or someone else.''

I was smoking a cigarette; she let her eyes inspect it. I fished out another for her, lighted it.

''Thanks,'' she said. ''Who is this Mick O'Rourke, Al?''

I smiled. ''Just a big bruiser who's been reading things—and likes it,'' I said. ''He's a funny case.''

She shook her head. ''He isn't funny,'' she corrected. ''And he isn't dumb—not the way I mean. What did Vennell want him aboard for, Al?''

I widened my eyes. ''Vennell—want Mick aboard?'' I said. ''What makes you think—''

Sonia shook her head sadly. ''You can't act, Al,'' she said. ''That sort of stuff is just as good as an answer.''

I frowned past her, toward the lights of the Jersey shore. There was a lot of boat traffic on the river; yachts were sailing downstream. Already there was a thinning out of the craft gathered for the Regatta.

I said suddenly, looking at Sonia squarely:

''You're pretty crazy over Tim Burke, Sonia?''

She started. Her body jerked a little, and her arms came away from the rail. Then she relaxed again.

''Tim's pretty swell,'' she said slowly.

I nodded. ''He rowed a nice race,'' I said. ''And he's a good, strong swimmer, too.''

Some of the color went out of her cheeks. She took

her gray eyes away from mine. Her slender, brown fingers tapped the rail.

"If Risdon asks me tough questions—ones that might hurt somebody—should I tell him the truth, Sonia?" I asked.

She didn't answer that one right away. And when she did answer it, her voice was very soft, and a little tired.

"Yes," she said.

I shrugged. I looked toward the California boathouse and half closed my eyes.

"That poor kid, Harron," I muttered. "Just at the peak of his college years. Just ready for—"

She closed her eyes and shook her head from side to side almost savagely. Her lips trembled a little, but she didn't speak. I looked away from her, and didn't look at her again until she said:

"What about Vennell?"

I shrugged. "He's hard," I said. "You know that—and I know it."

She said: "Why do you say *I* know it?"

"The *Virgin* was on the west coast, six months ago," I replied. "You come from California."

"What of that, Al?" she asked. "What's that got to do with my knowing he's hard?"

I lighted another cigarette from the glowing tip of the one that was almost finished.

"I've watched you—and I've watched Eric Vennell," I said. "I'm not a friend of his—when he invites me anywhere, there's a reason. And I've got a hunch he's that way with most people. It's always been Vennell first. I've seen him looking at you, watching you. And a couple of times I've seen you looking at him. You two know each other."

She sucked in her breath sharply. Then she sighed a little.

"But what about Vennell?" she asked again. "You

don't think he's dead. Mick O'Rourke doesn't think so, either. Babe Harron wasn't close to either of you. His death doesn't hit you very hard. But if you thought Vennell was dead, even though you hated him, you'd have acted differently.''

I said: ''That sounds like good reasoning.''

She nodded, her eyes serious. ''But you don't answer my question. What happened to Vennell?''

I shook my head. ''The last I saw of him he was sort of staggering along the deck, forward on the port side. There was a lot of wind and rain. I went after him—and I didn't find him.''

She said with an edge in her voice: ''*Why* did you go after him?''

I looked toward the Jersey shore for a few seconds. Then I said softly:

''You can ask the damndest questions, Sonia.''

She didn't reply. But her cool gray eyes were on mine.

''There was something I wanted to ask him,'' I said finally.

She nodded, her face set. ''How much he had lost on California?'' she asked.

I shook my head. ''No—I knew the answer to that one.''

Her eyes widened again. She spoke slowly.

''You knew how much?''

I nodded. ''He didn't lose a cent on California,'' I said quietly. ''And you know it.''

Her lips moved, but she didn't speak. She closed her eyes, and her body swayed a little. I said:

''You know what you're doing, Sonia—you're probably the coolest, sanest woman on the *Virgin*. But this spot is tough, and it's going to be tougher. I'd be—careful.''

She opened her eyes. ''Why did Eric want Mick O'Rourke as a bodyguard?'' she asked very steadily.

I smiled at her. "Why did Tim Burke swim out to the *Virgin* last night?" I said.

She took both arms away from the rail and stood very erect. She was breathing swiftly, and her face was very pale. For a second I saw fear in her eyes, and then it was gone. She got calm—very calm.

"You saw him," she said, and there was no questioning tone.

I nodded. "And I saw you," I said. "And I heard you talking with him."

She was silent. A boat whistle came from the far side of the Hudson. There was a very dull rumble of thunder. Then she spoke. Her voice was a little shaken, but clear.

"And *I* know that you brought O'Rourke aboard to protect Vennell," she said.

"That would be pretty hard to prove," I said quietly.

She nodded. "Perhaps. And it would be pretty hard to prove that Tim Burke swam to the *Virgin*."

I shook my head. "I don't think so—not with things started along those lines," I replied.

Once again I saw fear in her eyes. She touched my arm with the fingers of her right hand. She smiled a little and the fear went away.

"Well—what if Tim Burke *did* swim out to the yacht to see me?" she said defiantly.

I frowned. "I don't think it would be a nice thing for Risdon to know," I said.

She shook her head. "Of course it wouldn't. It wouldn't be pleasant—for me. It was long after midnight—"

She checked herself, flushed. I said:

"Don't feel bad about admitting it for the first time, Sonia. I knew he was here. I watched him swim back, and I heard you tell him to get started."

She said: "What are you going to do about it, Al?"

I frowned. "What shall I do?" I asked. "I certainly won't volunteer the information to Risdon. And if I'm asked directly—"

I hesitated. She said: "Well—what then?"

"It's up to you," I replied. "I've lied before in my life. And I expect to lie again. Lying for you would be a pleasure, only—"

"Only what?" she asked.

"There's a chance I'd get trapped. And that would make matters a lot worse."

She nodded her head very slowly. She said:

"I don't quite see how Risdon would force you to lie—about Tim."

I skipped my cigarette into the water. Faint lightning color showed momentarily in the western sky. It seemed to be getting warmer; there was little breeze.

"Risdon might not ask me," I said. "But someone else might."

Her keen eyes were looking into mine again. Her voice held a slight husky note.

"Who else?" she asked.

"Babe Harron is dead," I said. "Two doctors believe he was murdered. There's probably an autopsy on now. That'll decide. If it's murder, they'll work from the boat-house end, of course. And they won't miss much. Harron's father has all sorts of money. You think Tim Burke got away from his sleeping quarters and back again—without being seen?"

She shivered a little. Then she closed a fist and battered it into the palm of her other hand.

"Damn it!" she said fiercely. "Tim shouldn't have—come out."

I said grimly: "He certainly shouldn't—have come out here."

We were both silent for a little while. I looked down at the water; it was quite calm now. She spoke very softly, almost as though she were talking to herself. Her voice was toneless.

"Tim might have got out here—and back there—without being seen. There's a chance."

I shook my head. "I saw him," I corrected.

She said in a tone that was suddenly hard:

"But you said you'd lie for me."

I smiled. "Yes. But just at the time that Tim Burke left this yacht, Vennell's cabin was entered. And Carla Sard was moving around at that time."

Sonia drew in a sharp breath. She said:

"You think—she may have seen Tim? May have heard us?"

I frowned. "Why not?"

Sonia shook her head. "I don't think she did," she said slowly, softly.

We were both silent for several seconds. Then she said:

"A little while ago you said that Vennell didn't lose any money on California, and that *I* knew it."

I waited, but she didn't go on. She kept her eyes on mine. She said:

"What makes you think I knew it?"

I smiled a little. "There was the radiogram that you dropped when you ran up the companionway, after you told Tim Burke to get overboard," I said slowly.

Once again I saw fear in her eyes; her slender body was taut. She started to speak, but she didn't. I got another cigarette from my pack.

She said: "What radiogram?"

I made a clicking sound and shook my head.

"This isn't getting us anywhere, Sonia," I said. "You ask questions, and you already know the answers. I know them, too."

She said: "Just the same, I didn't drop any radiogram."

I nodded. "All right, you didn't drop any radiogram," I said. "But I found one. It was in code—and it was for Vennell. It wasn't the sort of thing that required a Van Dine character to decipher. Even I got the answer."

Sonia said grimly: "And then you knew that Vennell wasn't betting on California?"

I nodded. "And you knew it—before I did," I said.

She didn't deny that. But she said very thoughtfully: "I sensed it."

"Why?" I asked.

She looked serious. "Vennell is a gambler—and he likes the odds against him. When he wins, he likes to win big."

I nodded. "And Vennell lost a lot of money lately," I said. "There were a lot of crews in this race—and he couldn't be too sure of the favorite. So he just went and picked a long shot."

Sonia said: "Navy?"

"That would have been tough," I replied. "But it would have been nice if he'd picked Columbia, wouldn't it?"

She said: "Did he?"

I looked her in the eyes. "You've brains," I said. "What did you figure from that radiogram?"

She spoke steadily. "I never had a radiogram, Al—I swear to that. I didn't drop it."

I believed her. I wanted to believe her, and probably that made it easier.

"All right," I said. "Well, I figure Vennell had an awful lot of money on Columbia. He was getting pretty nervous. He was worried, maybe about other things besides the bet. It looked as though California was going to win—but Columbia did the trick. I caught a glimpse of his face as he turned away from the rail. It wasn't pretty to look at."

Sonia Vreedon's eyes were narrowed. She said huskily: "Why not—if he'd won?"

"It didn't look as though he were going to win—until the last minute," I replied slowly. "Vennell got a jolt. It takes a few seconds to recover."

Sonia had her gray eyes almost closed. She said in almost a whisper:

"Then what happened—to Vennell?"

I shook my head. A steward came along the deck calling:

"Mr. Connors—Mr. Connors—"

I said: "Here!"

He came up close to us and smiled at me. He was short and ruddy-faced.

"Mr. Risdon would like to see you in the captain's quarters, sir."

I nodded and he went away. Sonia touched my wrist. Her fingers were cool.

"I think—it had better be the truth, Al," she said softly.

I nodded. "Tim Burke's—a lucky guy," I replied. "It'll be the truth, Sonia."

She smiled a little, and there was color in her cheeks. I turned away and followed the steward toward the bridge. A radio or phonograph on a passing yacht was playing "Little White Lies." I shook my head and went inside of the captain's quarters.

2

Latham was seated on a small window seat, his body sprawled a bit. Risdon sat behind a desk on which were a lot of papers. He was smoking a thin cigar and had a pencil in his right-hand fingers. Mick O'Rourke leaned against the far wall of the room. The big fellow was grinning.

I said: "Hello—this looks like business."

The captain said nothing. Risdon cleared his throat and got a vacant stare in his eyes. They didn't look so green in the light of the cabin. Mick said:

"Funny business, Al."

Risdon gestured toward a chair and I went over and used it. He said:

"Before I ask some questions, understand this, Connors. There may be a connection between the disappearance of Eric Vennell—and the murder of this stroke, Harron."

I widened my eyes. "Autopsy finished?" I said. "It is murder, then?"

Risdon shook his head. "I haven't got word," he replied. "But I saw Harron at the boathouse. I got word that something was wrong, and I was on the Highland side of the river. I went down. He has the mark of a hypodermic needle just to the right of his left shoulder blade, up pretty high. It's the only mark on his body. The chief and I were talking when Captain Latham's messenger reached the Poughkeepsie police station. Talking on the phone. He told me to come out."

I didn't say anything. Mick O'Rourke said:

"Supposin' some guy got shot, down in New York, at just about the time Harron keeled over, and Vennell disappeared—do you figure he's mixed up in it, too?"

Risdon smiled coldly. "The more you talk, the more I like it," he said. "The first thing you know, you'll say the wrong thing."

Mick said: "Jees—I never thought of that."

Risdon looked at me and spoke in a casual tone. He kept his eyes partially closed.

"O'Rourke says he's an ex-actor and an ex-prizefighter. He says you run a column for a New York newspaper, and he furnishes you most of the stuff that goes into it."

I grinned at Mick. "Most of the *funny* stuff," I agreed.

Risdon nodded. "He says Vennell wanted you along on the yacht because you were old friends, and that you brought him along because you wanted to keep writing the column."

I nodded. "That's about right," I said.

Risdon tapped an end of his pencil against the desk surface.

"I wouldn't lie, Connors," he advised. "This is serious business."

Mick said with sarcasm: "Sure—maybe Vennell's dead. You can't tell."

Captain Latham spoke. "Connors was somewhere prowling around the decks when Vennell's cabin was broken into last night," he said calmly.

I nodded. "That's right," I agreed. "It looks like I burn for the job."

Risdon snapped: "What were you doing on deck after three in the morning?"

I grinned at him. "Couldn't sleep—went out for a little air."

He made some notes. Mick chuckled.

"What a bright young district attorney could do to those lines, Al!" he muttered.

Captain Latham frowned. Risdon kept scratching on the paper. I relaxed in the chair. After a few seconds Risdon looked up at me and said:

"Well, while you were wandering around the decks at three in the morning—did you see anything unusual?"

I thought that over. "What do you mean by unusual?" I asked. "Everything was more or less unusual to me. A yacht isn't like Broadway, Harlem—or the Village."

Risdon slapped down his pencil and leaned forward in his chair. His greenish eyes got down to little points.

"You don't seem to want to help me much, any of you," he said. "With the exception of Jones you're all evading my questions."

Mick said: "By God—that's it! Torry's innocent, and the rest of us are guilty."

Risdon pointed a finger at him. "Now you just shut your mouth, big boy!" he said in a hard voice. "I've heard enough from you."

Mick O'Rourke stopped leaning against the wall. He took two steps forward, stopped. His long arms were swinging a little at his sides, and his big head had dropped forward a little.

"Listen, Risdon," he said huskily—"I don't take it from hick dicks like you! You talk to me like that again and I'll chuck you overboard!"

Risdon made a swift movement with his left hand. His gun looked like a thirty-eight Smith and Wesson. He held it for a second, then set it on the table. He kept his eyes on Mick.

I said: "What's that—a rod?"

Mick's face was twisting. His fingers were clenched at his sides; he stared at the gun. Then suddenly he relaxed. A slow smiled spread over his big face. The scar stopped twitching.

"Jees, Al—I guess he *is* a detective," he said with awe in his voice. "He's carrying a gun, all right."

I nodded. "Sure he is," I said. "We'd better be good, Mick."

The big fellow backed up and leaned against the far wall again. Latham looked at me and said slowly:

"It seems peculiar to me—most of Mr. Vennell's guests don't appear anxious to help matters any. He invited them aboard, and yet—"

I cut in. "That's right—he invited us aboard, Captain. Yet none of us knew him very well."

Latham looked puzzled. "Mr. Vennell was not one who had many intimate friends," he said.

Risdon looked down at his notes. "I'll get what I want, Captain," he said softly. "Don't worry about that."

Mick grunted. "You can't say a Risdon doesn't get his man," he breathed. "No, sir!"

The detective paid no attention to the big fellow. Risdon looked at me.

"You heard screams while you were on deck, Connors?" he asked.

I nodded. He said: "You stayed on deck for a few minutes *after* you heard them?"

I nodded again. "For a few minutes," I said.

"See anybody else on deck?" he asked.

I hesitated. It was strange the way I felt about Sonia Vreedon. But I felt that way. I could see her leaning against the yacht rail, her eyes wide on mine. I could see the fear in them. But she had wanted the truth given.

I said: "Yes."

Risdon waited, and when I didn't speak, he said: "Who?"

I looked toward a port behind the detective. Latham and Mick were very quiet.

"Miss Vreedon," I said very slowly.

Latham straightened his sprawled body a little. Mick muttered: "Huh?"

Risdon said: "Miss Vreedon, eh?"

I nodded. Mick looked at me and said very huskily: "What the hell, Al?"

I shrugged. "Harron's dead, and Vennell's missing," I reminded. "I'm telling what I know. Just so long as I'm treated right—"

Risdon was scratching on a piece of paper. He looked at the captain.

"What's her first name, Captain?" he asked.

Latham said: "Sonia Vreedon."

Risdon put down his pencil and took the thin cigar from his mouth. He inspected the end that wasn't lighted as though it were something very curious.

"Sonia Vreedon," he repeated. "That's the girl that Jones told me was engaged to a fellow named Burke, Number Seven on the California crew—the varsity."

Latham said: "I believe she is, Risdon."

The detective got the cigar back in his mouth.

Risdon said thoughtfully: "Number Seven is right ahead of the stroke in a shell, isn't he?"

Latham said grimly: "He sure is."

Risdon said: "Not much of a reach—to touch the stroke on the shoulder, say."

I looked at the ceiling of the captain's living room and tried to keep my face expressionless. Risdon stopped thinking and using his imagination. He leaned forward and got his greenish eyes on me again.

"See anybody *else* on deck at about the time you saw the Vreedon girl?" he asked.

I shook my head. Risdon said: "Well, now—what do you suppose—"

He checked himself, and I could see by his eyes that he had the big idea. He said grimly:

"See anyone in the water, Connors?"

I said: "I'd like to answer your questions, Risdon—but I think maybe you'd better ask them with just you and me in here."

Latham frowned. Mick said again:

"What the hell, Al!"

Risdon nodded his head slowly. "Just you and me in here, eh?" he said. "All right, Connors."

Captain Latham stood up, still frowning. He went toward the door that led to the corridor that led to the deck. Mick followed him slowly. Risdon said:

"You stick aboard ship, Mr. O'Rourke."

Mick smiled at him. "I'll bet you shoot straight and fast, Mr. Risdon," he replied.

They both went out. I listened to Mick's big feet making noise on the linoleum of the corridor. Risdon sat back in his chair and waited. After a little while he spoke in a pleasant voice.

"Just who is this Mick O'Rourke, Connors?"

I shrugged. "Until lately he's been a sort of body guard for a big New York businessman," I said. "Mick's all right."

Risdon smiled, but not so pleasantly. He fingered his pencil.

"What sort of a businessman?" he asked.

I shook my head. "I don't remember his line," I lied. "But I think he'd made his money in the Middle West."

Risdon smiled coldly. "Maybe in Chicago," he guessed.

I said: "Perhaps."

The detective stood up and rubbed his hands together. They made a pleasant swishing sound, the way he did it.

"Maybe this big businessman was in the wet-goods line?" Risdon guessed again.

I lied again. "I don't remember."

Risdon came around and sat on the edge of the table. He kept some of the weight on his feet.

"Who did you see in the water, Connors—just after you heard the screams?"

I looked him in the eyes. "Someone that had just been called Tim Burke, Risdon," I said. "Rather, he'd just been called Tim."

Risdon said: "Ah—"

I shook my head. "Get this straight. Sonia Vreedon and Burke were aft when the screams came. I was near them, though I didn't know who they were at the time. The screams gave them as much of a jolt as they did me. It was then that Sonia told Burke to get away from the yacht."

Risdon just kept narrowed eyes on mine. I said slowly:

"I wanted to tell you this alone, because I think it was just one of those things. Burke hadn't seen the girl for quite a while. He knew the yacht was out here—he'd seen it. I guess he's pretty crazy over her. He must have taken a big chance—he swam out."

The detective said: "Yeah? You think that was it?"

I nodded. The more I saw of Risdon, the more I was convinced that he had brains. A nice set of them.

"I came through with the truth, because you might have got at it anyway, Risdon. And I wanted you to have it straight. I don't think it means anything. Just a tough piece of luck—for Burke and the girl."

Risdon said: "I know something about crew, Connors. I've pulled an oar myself. I stick close to all the regattas around here, and I know most of the coaches. It's sort of hobby with me. You think it's a cinch for a Number Seven in a varsity shell to get away from his sleeping quarters at three in the morning of the day of the race—and swim to a yacht and get back—without being seen?"

I shook my head. "No—because he *was* seen," I said. "But if I hadn't gone on deck for air—"

Risdon cut in sharply: "You don't think he might have been seen at the *other* end, eh?"

I didn't answer that one. The detective smiled at me with tight lips. He parted them.

"You were pretty *sure* he might have been seen at the boathouse end," he said grimly. "And you held out on me until you figured you'd better talk fast."

I said: "Sonia Vreedon isn't a fool. But I didn't want her mixed up in a silly—"

Risdon raised his thin eyebrows. I shrugged. He relighted the dead end of his cigar.

"I'm staying on board the yacht, Connors," he said. "So are the rest of you. I've sent word ashore—there's some information I want. It can be got from New York. Vennell may not be dead, but something's wrong. It's wrong here—and it's wrong over at the California quarters. And there might be a line between the two."

I sighed. "Go easy with Sonia Vreedon," I advised. "Her father is—"

"I've heard of him," Risdon cut in. He smiled almost cheerfully. "How do you suppose she and Tim Burke pulled off that meeting so smoothly, Connors?"

I widened my eyes. "Smoothly?" I asked.

But he was getting at the thing I didn't want him to get at.

He nodded. "Smoothly," he repeated. "The *Virgin*'s a pretty fair-sized boat. It was after three. Do you suppose Burke just swam out—and there was Miss Vreedon, stargazing somewhere aft? Or do you think she went for a swim, too—and they just happened to meet somewhere along the line?''

I said: ''I don't know, Risdon.''

His face got hard. ''You know, Connors,'' he said slowly, ''there just *might* have been some sort of an arrangement.''

I didn't answer that one, either. He expected me to answer it—his eyes held mine. He said:

''And if there was an arrangement—when was it made?''

I rubbed the knuckles of my left hand with the tips of right-hand fingers and said nothing. Risdon stood up and drew in a deep breath.

''I'll have to talk with Miss Vreedon,'' he said quietly.

I got up, too. ''She won't mind it too much,'' I said. ''After all, what it amounts to is that Vennell has lost a lot of money on the Street. His nerves are shot. Maybe he wanted California to win pretty badly. When the crew lost, he went crazy—''

Risdon swore at me: ''*I* won't go crazy, Connors,'' he said grimly. ''And *you* won't go crazy.''

I said: ''Thanks. And Mick won't go crazy.''

The lean-faced detective narrowed his greenish eyes.

''If he does,'' he said very softly, ''he'll go crazy like a fox.''

I smiled a little. ''If you give him—''

There was a hoarse shout from the corridor beyond the captain's quarters. There was the sound of footfalls—and they were swift ones. Someone was running. A voice called jerkily:

''Captain Latham—Captain Latham!''

I started for the door, but Risdon was ahead of me. He got it opened. Griggs was outside, his face white except where it was splotched with red. He was breathing with difficulty.

He said: ''Is Captain Latham—''

Risdon said: ''He's not here—what's wrong?''

Griggs stared at me. He said hoarsely:

"Mr. Vennell—forward—lying on the deck—"

I said: "Dead?"

Griggs sucked in a deep breath. He was getting more color in his cheeks now.

"I don't know," he breathed. "He's—unconscious!"

Risdon was out in the corridor, moving toward the deck. I followed him, and Griggs came along behind me. I noticed a small searchlight playing across the *Virgin*, aft, as we ran forward. It seemed to come from a launch that was approaching the yacht. Risdon stumbled on something and almost went down. I was at his side; he reached out a hand and gripped my right arm.

"You stay—*back* of me, Connors!" he snapped.

Griggs said huskily: "Up there—near the anchor chain."

I saw Mick O'Rourke's big body first. It was straightening up, slowly, as we got near him. Then I saw the figure of Eric Vennell, stretched on the wood of the deck. Risdon looked at Mick and said grimly:

"How'd *you* get here—in such a hurry?"

Mick said tonelessly: "I heard Griggs yelling—"

Griggs said: "I didn't yell, sir."

Risdon bent over the figure of the yacht owner. His eyes were narrowed. Mick said slowly:

"He's hurt, but he ain't dead."

Vennell moved his arms and groaned. His voice sounded, thick and weak.

"I won't pay—you took the chance—I won't pay . . ."

The words went off into a mumble. The yacht owner's body was motionless again. I said:

"Get Doctor Bryce, Griggs—make it fast!"

Risdon straightened and frowned at me. I looked down at Vennell. His clothes were soaked. His hair was mussed and clinging to his forehead. There was a thin line of red across his left ear. Water was making a puddle around his body.

Mick said grimly: "Looks as though he just came out of the river."

Risdon kept his eyes slitted on those of the big fellow. He said very softly:

"You don't miss a thing, O'Rourke."

•7•

MORPHINE

WHEN I went into the smoke room, Carla Sard was talking with Don Rayne. Rayne was saying:

"Vennell's a husky man for his age. If he put up a fight, the chances are the other fellow has marks. And if he regains consciousness, gives us a description—"

He heard me and stopped speaking. Carla was very pale, and she looked swell. Rayne frowned at me and said:

"Heard anything in the last ten minutes?"

I nodded. My lighter was dry and flameless, so I swiped a box of matches from one of the smoke-room tables. I offered cigarettes, and Carla said she was too nervous to smoke. She said it with a gesture, but I didn't applaud because it didn't strike me as being very clever. Don Rayne smiled at her and let his eyes show her he liked the idea.

I said: "A man named Crozier has just come aboard. He flew up from New York. Babe Harron's father sent him up. He's a detective."

Carla groaned. "*Another* one?" she murmured.

I said: "You'll like this chap. He's suave and very

cold and superior. He's the kind you read about in the books whose writers go in for annotations and such stuff. He's a friend of Harron's father."

Don Rayne squared his broad shoulders nervously, hunched them forward, and squared them again. It was a little habit he had; it almost seemed like a mild setting-up exercise.

"How about Vennell?" he asked.

"Still unconscious," I said.

Carla sighed. "It's all very terrible," she said. "I wish I'd gone to Lashinski's party, on Long Island."

I lighted a cigarette. Don Rayne said:

"If this Crozier was sent up by Babe Harron's father—what's he doing on the yacht?"

I shrugged. "He's talking to Sonia right now."

Carla sighed very heavily. "Poor Sonia," she said. "With Tim Burke on the losing crew—"

That wasn't what she meant, but it was what she said. I looked at Rayne.

"You're a crew man," I said. "Much chance of another man in a shell using a hypodermic needle on the man ahead of him?"

Rayne shook his head. "Two hands on the wood of his oar—got to be," he replied. "There's the slide rig motion to beat. Certainly he'd be seen. And where the devil would he hide the needle?"

"They're not very large," I reminded.

Rayne shook his head. "I don't believe the murder theory," he said in a superior manner. "It's wrong from a lot of angles. Coach may say that Harron's heart was fine. Maybe he thought it. But he overstrained. Columbia was coming up, and Ed Dale called for a stroke pickup. Harron tried and couldn't make it. That's my idea. Bad heart."

I said: "You know damn well that Columbia wasn't coming up—not until Harron started to go to pieces. I doubt if there was any stroke pickup until Dale tried to make a save. And there had been a heart examination, only a week or so ago."

Rayne shrugged. "It doesn't always show. They give fighters a stethoscope examination before they get into the ring. And every once in a while one of them goes out—without being hit much."

I said: "How about the mark on Harron's back, Rayne?"

He shrugged. "I've had little marks on my back, too. And then, again, Mears doesn't like to lose. He isn't used to it. No coach likes it much. He's lost his head and is looking for alibis."

I said: "And the crew doctor, Vollmer—he's helping him out by making a fool of himself, too?"

Rayne said: "After all, he's the California crew doctor."

Carla nodded her head and looked wise. "I think Don's right," she said. "It's a terrible thing—but Eric Vennell—*he's* the one—"

Her voice faltered and she shivered a little. I said to Don Rayne, keeping my voice low:

"Risdon got word from the Poughkeepsie police station. They held the autopsy an hour ago, at Vassar Hospital. Babe Harron died from poison— morphine in a large dose."

Carla Sard said: "Oh, God—"

Rayne swore very softly and stared at me. I looked at the tip of my cigarette.

"The morphine was injected near his left shoulder blade."

Rayne lifted his right hand, got it behind him. I smiled at him.

"It can be done," I said. "At least Vollmer says it can be. But he doesn't believe it could be done so cleanly. And why would Harron want to suicide *that* way?"

Rayne let his hand drop again. Carla Sard said shakily:

"Then it—was murder?"

"The coroner's jury will probably bring in that sort of a verdict tomorrow," I replied.

Carla Sard said very shakily: "Babe Harron murdered, morphined! And Eric Vennell attacked, knocked unconscious. He must have been unconscious a long time—yet he got back aboard the yacht."

I said: "Don't be silly, Carla. It's almost four hours since Vennell disappeared. He's been in the water, certainly, but that doesn't mean he's been unconscious a long time."

Carla said: "It's been that terrible man—the one in black, with the mask. The one who attacked me, last night. And he may be one of us, aboard—"

I said brutally: "You're still sticking to that story, Carla?"

Her eyes got wide. Don Rayne narrowed his.

"What do you mean by that, Connors?" he snapped.

I smiled at him. "You'd better be careful of Torry, Don," I said. "Carla's his gal."

Carla stood up. "Like hell I am!" she flared.

I said: "It isn't Mick O'Rourke you're crazy about?"

She started to wave her arms and to talk loudly. Rayne said:

"Cut it out, Carla. Connors is kidding you. They'll hear you, and there are a lot of strange people aboard. They won't know—"

He stopped. Carla kept her eyes narrowed on mine. She said coldly:

"It's a remarkable time to joke."

I shook my head. "Wasn't exactly joking, Carla. What I was trying to get across was that you might think over that scream story of yours. Risdon isn't a fool—and this fellow Crozier doesn't seem to be one. I'd be a little careful, that's all."

She laughed harshly. "I don't know what you're getting at, Mr. Connors," she said.

I nodded. ''All right—but Risdon knows what he's getting at,'' I returned. ''And I've got a sweet hunch that Crozier knows what he's getting at.''

Rayne said: ''You don't believe Carla? You think the masked man didn't run into her?''

I grinned at him. ''Was there a masked man, Rayne?'' I asked. ''Or was it love?''

Carla said: ''Good Lord—what a party this is turning out to be! Everyone suspicious of everyone else. It's just like—''

''I know the name of the play you mean,'' I said. ''And it's just like a couple of books, too.''

Don Rayne said grimly: ''And a hell of a lot of movies, too.''

I nodded. ''Just a sort of Make-Believe game, eh, Rayne?''

He looked puzzled. Carla closed her saucer eyes and touched her lovely hair with tapered finger-tips.

''It doesn't seem real,'' she breathed.

Mick O'Rourke's voiced sounded, heavy and grim, from some spot behind me.

''Maybe it's a dream and you'll wake up in the electric chair, kid.''

Carla opened her eyes and said: ''You address me differently! You understand?''

Mick said: ''Sure, kid.''

Carla stamped her right foot. Mick lifted one of his feet, and when he put it down, things rattled. Carla looked furious. I said:

''Careful—you'll put it through the keel.''

Carla Sard stood stiffly and held her head high. She looked swell.

Mick said: ''You look swell.''

She said icily: ''I'm going ashore—I'll go to the Nelson House, in Poughkeepsie.''

Mick grinned. ''Dive off the front of the boat, and the

tide'll help you along,'' he said. ''It's running strong. Look out for sharks.''

I frowned at him. ''The plural is similar to the singular, Mick. 'Look out for the shark.' ''

He took my right hand and shook it with enthusiasm. He nodded his big head.

''That's how I'm going to get ahead,'' he said in a determined voice. ''It's you that's givin' me my start, Al.''

There was contempt in Carla's eyes. Don Rayne still looked puzzled. He was watching Mick very closely.

I said: ''It seems to me the little things can assume considerable importance in the greater scheme of things.''

Mick nodded. ''As one of the noblest Romans has said—translated roughly—'' he started, but Carla interrupted.

''And Eric Vennell may be dying!'' she said in a tragic voice.

Mick said: ''He's not—he's just a little out of his head. I've been the same way.''

Carla said: ''For years.''

Mick bowed. ''You're fast, kid,'' he said in a tone that held exaggerated admiration. ''You've got a certain—''

He stopped, shook his head. He said: ''You've got that—you give me a feeling of—''

He stopped again, shook his head. Carla was standing stiffly, her eyes calm. I said:

''The Greeks had a word for it, Mick.''

His face lighted. ''That's it!'' he breathed. ''Jees, yes—sure.''

He looked at Carla, then frowned again. ''You are familiar with the Greeks, Miss Sard?'' he asked.

I said sharply: ''Of course not.''

But Carla had gone Hollywood now. She was being that way and using her brains.

"Thank you for defending me, Mr. Connors," she said coldly. "But it happens I am familiar with Mr. Schnesi, the millionaire importer. He is a Greek."

I bowed. Mick said: "Well, maybe you know the word they had for it, then?"

She nodded. "It goes for *you*, too, Mr. O'Rourke," she said evenly. " 'Lousy'—wasn't it?"

She walked past me and past Mick. She went along the corridor with her head held high, and she looked like a million, from the rear.

Mick scratched his chin and whistled softly. He stopped whistling.

"She said that like she meant it, Al," he muttered.

Rayne said with fine sarcasm: "She doesn't understand you, Mr. O'Rourke."

The big fellow frowned. "You think that's it? I'm simple, too. Easy to figure."

Rayne moved over close to me. He kept his eyes on mine when he spoke.

"An automatic's simple, too," he said. "And easy to figure."

He went from the smoke room. Mick and I were silent for a few seconds. Then the big fellow said:

"The yacht's getting visitors. And things are getting a little tight."

I nodded. "You worrying any?" I asked.

Mick looked surprised. "Me worrying?" he breathed. His voice got a little hard. "Not yet, Al."

I said: "When do you start?"

He drew a deep breath and spread his arms. He took up a lot of space in the room. When he expelled the breath, there was a whistling sound. He smiled and then his mouth got tight and his eyes smaller.

"I don't like the looks of this guy Crozier," he said. "He looks like a gent that starts something with the idea of finishing it."

I nodded. "He's cool, intelligent—and tough-brained.

He's not being worried much about Vennell—he's working from the Harron end.''

Mick frowned. ''Just the same—when Vennell starts to talk—we're going to learn something.''

I said: ''Sure—something.''

The big fellow looked at me sharply. There was a little silence.

''Listen, Al—'' he said softly—''you still think I may be crossing you up, eh?''

I stared at him and got amazement in my voice.

''*You* crossing anyone up, Mick?'' I breathed. ''How in hell could anyone think *that*?''

He said: ''It beats me. But even that Rayne fellow acts suspicious.''

I shook my head as though it were almost unbelievable.

''With your open face!'' I muttered.

A voice somewhere beyond the smoke room said in a fairly loud tone:

''—and instruct the captain not to get this yacht under way.''

Mick groaned. ''I hope the food holds out,'' he said.

I smiled at him and decided that he was just one of the people on board who was lying. I figured that Carla Sard was another. Vennell I knew had lied. Torry Jones was coming close to it. And even Sonia Vreedon—

Mick's voice broke in on my line of thought. He said:

''It's queer about Vennell. A little bump on the head—and he can't seem to come out of it.''

''It's—damn queer,'' I agreed.

The big fellow frowned toward the floor.

''When you can't talk—there's not much use of guys askin' you questions,'' he observed, after a little while.

I smiled grimly. ''That's a fact,'' I said.

2

Crozier was a well built man of about forty. He had a gray mustache and gray hair, and small, firm features. His eyes were pale blue and very clear. When he tapped on the door of Suite B, I let him in. He closed the door behind him.

"I'm Mel Crozier," he said in an unhurried tone. "You're Connors, I believe."

I nodded and we shook hands. I'd stood close to him before, and I'd heard him talk. He was very direct, and yet he didn't rush things. He looked at Mick, who was standing near a port behind his bed.

"And you're O'Rourke," he said, slowly, smiling a little. "A couple of good Irish names."

I said: "Just a couple more like Mick—and we'd have a Notre Dame backfield."

Crozier nodded, still smiling. Then he went over to a chair and sat down. I picked out another, but Mick stayed on his feet. Crozier said:

"Babe Harron's father is a friend of mine. This is a pretty rotten thing."

His face was serious suddenly. I said:

"It's a damn shame."

Crozier nodded. "Jones, Captain Latham, a Rita Velda, and a Carla Sard—they all seem to think that you and O'Rourke here are taking things pretty lightly."

I nodded. "It's a matter of temperament," I said. "I'm a newspaperman, and I've seen a lot of people have things happen to them. Somehow, I can't get completely broken up because someone I've never been within ten feet of is murdered."

Crozier nodded. "You been that close to Babe Harron?" he asked.

I shook my head. "Not that I know of," I said. "Not within fifty feet of him."

Crozier looked at Mick. "It's like this, Connors," he said in his unhurried tone, "I'm up here for Harron's father. He has a big business—and I normally investigate his employees for him. The ones that he may want to make important. I'm not a detective. Babe Harron has been morphined to death. The general opinion of three doctors and the coach seems to be that the morphine was injected just under the left shoulder, a short time before the varsity crew got away from the boathouse. It was intended to take effect sooner, but there was almost a mistake. The effort of stroking the crew slowed down the effects of the morphine, kept it from numbing his body, reaching the heart. If Harron had been sitting round somewhere, or sleeping, it would have killed him sooner. It was a strong dose. Hitting him as it did, the chances are he simply felt a numbness—everything in his body slowed up. He might have thought he had pulled himself out—and then he collapsed. The morphine had reached his heart."

Crozier paused. He said: "You've got a man out here—this Eric Vennell—who seems to have been afraid of something. I've asked a lot of questions, and I've answered a lot. I'm out here because one of the boys in the crew saw another boy—Tim Burke—leave the boathouse, shortly after three last night."

I nodded. Crozier smiled a little.

"I believe you were on deck when Vennell's suite was entered by this mysterious masked man," he said. "You saw Burke swimming back."

I nodded. "Risdon's being quite frank with you, Mr. Crozier," I said.

He stopped smiling. "I hope so. I've talked with a Miss Vreedon. She answers certain of my questions, but she refuses to answer the ones I consider most important. She insists that Burke simply took a chance—to see her. She happened to be on deck, and he found her. They talked a little—there were screams. He dove in and swam back. The same crew man who had seen him sneak out saw him come back."

I frowned. "He didn't speak to Burke about it?" I asked.

Crozier said: "Yes, he did. It was Johnny Light, who pulled Number Two oar. He bawled Burke out—he knew he had a girl aboard the yacht, and it was his idea that the swim, loss of sleep, and whatnot had not helped Burke any—with the big race coming up in about fourteen hours."

Mick said slowly: "Well, Burke seemed to be all right in the race."

Crozier nodded. "Fourteen hours is a long time. He was in perfect physical shape, and it wasn't much of a swim. The crew doctor, Vollmer—he admits it wouldn't hurt much. But that was Light's theory, anyway."

I said: "And when it became known that Babe Harron had been morphined to death—this fellow Light made his guess about where Burke had been?"

Crozier said: "He answered questions. When he got to the one about seeing anything unusual, he mentioned Tim Burke's getting away. We went to Burke. At first he denied it, tried to laugh it off. Then he admitted he'd made the swim. At first he refused to name the girl—finally he did that. He was very upset and said he was in love with her, hadn't seen her for quite some time, and simply had to get out here. He didn't expect to find her on deck—that had been luck. He had hardly commenced talking with her when there were screams—and she asked him to get away. He did. That's all he knew."

Crozier passed the cigarettes. I said: "You've talked with Sonia?"

He nodded. "Her story agrees with his. She won't tell me the real reason for her being on deck at three in the morning, and she says she can't remember the exact conversation between herself and Burke."

Mick said: "Well—maybe she forgot it."

I said: "There wasn't much reason for my being on deck, Crozier. I couldn't sleep, that's all—and felt that I wanted some air."

He said grimly. "You're a man—you can do things a woman would hesitate to do."

I shook my head. "Convention wouldn't stop Sonia," I said. "If she felt like going on deck, she'd go."

Crozier looked at me steadily. "All right," he said. "Now, here's the point. Babe Harron's skin was burned brown by the sun, of course. The mark of the hypodermic syringe needle is quite small. It would be difficult for the other crew men to spot. Or the coach. But in the autopsy it was determined that the injection was pretty crude. The needle could have been used by an expert so it would have left a much smaller mark. And there are better spots for injection."

I said: "He might have been sleeping with his left shoulder exposed, when he got the injection."

Crozier said grimly: "The needle would have wakened him—but that isn't what I'm getting at. We know Harron was murdered, morphined."

Mick said: "Yeah—he could have stuck himself, couldn't he?"

Crozier looked at Mick with his clear, blue eyes slightly narrowed.

"It would be difficult—self-injection in such a spot. Harron had everything to live for. Everything. He was all right in his studies; he had the advantages of wealth. He had friends. If there was something we haven't found out about—and if he did suicide—why such a method? And if such a method, why such a spot?"

I said: "So it wouldn't look like suicide."

Crozier frowned at me. "The coroner's verdict will be murder—official tomorrow," he said. "What I want is Babe Harron's killer."

Mick said: "And you think he's on the yacht?"

Crozier looked at me. "One of Doctor Vollmer's hypo needles is missing," he said slowly. "It was in a case with others of different size, yesterday morning. None of the morphine is gone, but that isn't difficult to get."

I whistled softly. Mick muttered something that I didn't catch.

Crozier said: "What I want to know is why Tim Burke swam out here—and what happened after he got here."

"He swam out here to see Sonia Vreedon," I said. "There was some excitement—and he left in a hurry."

Crozier nodded. "What caused the excitement?"

I said: "Somebody broke into Vennell's room."

Crozier said: "What for?"

I shrugged. "Vennell is known to have a lot of diamonds. He's a wealthy man. One of the crew, perhaps, saw a chance—or thought he saw one."

Crozier looked at Mick O'Rourke. He said very slowly:

"I've heard the reason why you're supposed to be aboard, O'Rourke. It's not as good a one as the one you had for being close to Andy Dormer, before he got careless and then got killed."

Mick's body moved a little, jerkily. Crozier ran fingers through his gray hair. He smiled almost gently. He said:

"Vennell's a gambler. He's lost a lot of money lately. Never heard of him caring much about Regatta stuff, before this year. He's got a strange crowd aboard this boat. A mixed crowd. Two newspapermen. Wonder if he did any betting on the race."

I said: "He said he had a pretty good bet—on California."

Crozier shook his head. "Too bad," he breathed. "That's tough."

Mick said slowly: "If it's a murder—maybe bets will be called off."

Crozier shook his head. "California was rowing a sweet race, until right at the finish. And murder hasn't been proved. The bets go—and Columbia goes into the records as the winner.''

Mick looked at the ceiling of the suite. Crozier kept his eyes on the big fellow.

''For one reason or another, Eric Vennell wanted you aboard as a bodyguard, O'Rourke,'' he said slowly. ''You haven't been exactly—up to scratch.''

Mick looked at me. I said: ''Vennell didn't want O'Rourke as a bodyguard, Crozier. He wanted a bodyguard. *I* got O'Rourke.''

Mick stared at me. Crozier didn't look too surprised. He just nodded his head. I said:

''You seem pretty square—I'll tell you some things. Vennell called me and asked me to pick a good man. My column means that I mix around some. I picked Mick, here. Vennell had a talk with us and told us he was on the spot. He was the silent partner of a certain brokerage house on the Street. Money was lost in the house, by a partner who took racket coin. Not lost by him—he did what he was told. But the losers figured Vennell should make up the loss. They got word to him, and he said no. They told him he'd better. Then he called me and got up this yacht trip. The Regatta gave him an excuse to get away. He wanted a bodyguard, so I got Mick.''

Crozier nodded almost pleasantly. I went over to my biggest piece of luggage and opened it. When I came away from it, I handed Crozier the business card I'd found on the smoke-room floor—and the radiogram that had been on the companionway step. I told him about them.

Mick said, when I got through: ''You may be making a mistake, Al.''

Crozier looked at him sharply. ''He's not,'' he said quietly. ''When there's murder—truth is a good thing to share.''

I said: "Sometimes."

If Crozier heard me, he gave no evidence of it. He had finished with the business card; his blue eyes were on the radiogram. I sat down and waited, Mick stood near the port and frowned at me. After a few minutes Crozier looked up and said:

"I'm getting stupid—it shouldn't have taken me that long. It's pretty obvious."

I said: "Sure."

Crozier said: "Well—Vennell *wasn't* betting on California. He had his money on Columbia. A lot of it. He got odds. Tim Burke came out here last night. He rowed ahead of Babe Harron. Harron was morphined and collapsed. California lost. Columbia won. Vennell cleaned up. Then he disappeared. He was found unconscious and apparently hit on the head, his body soaked, on the deck—after four hours. Bryce says he doesn't seem to be badly hurt, but he can't seem to talk. He mutters the same half-phrases over and over—something about not paying somebody. And apparently he had been put on the spot. I've got a card here that's a warning, or a note. Reddish ink—very perfect handwriting—"

He stopped talking. His eyes smiled a little, into mine.

Mick said: "You didn't tell me Vennell was betting on Columbia, Al."

I said: "Didn't I? I'm sorry, Mick."

"Like hell you are!" he gritted.

Crozier stood up. He said: "Mind if I keep the business card—and the radiogram?"

I shook my head. "Risdon doesn't know about either of them," I said. "I was going a little easy with him—he acted as though he might go at things pretty roughly. And I've got an idea that might not work so well."

Crozier nodded. "Agreed," he said. "For a little while we'll keep these two things under cover. Anyone else know about them, besides the three of us?"

I said: "Vennell knows about the card—I showed it to him. And Sonia Vreedon knows about the radiogram."

The gray-haired one widened his blue eyes. "Sonia Vreedon?" he said. "Why does she know about it?"

I smiled at him. "I thought she might have dropped it," I said steadily. "I found it just after Tim Burke dove from the yacht, and Sonia came up the companionway steps."

Crozier said: "Well—"

I shook my head. "She hadn't dropped it—she hadn't seen it," I said firmly.

The gray-haired one said slowly: "How do you know that, Connors?"

"She told me that," I said.

Crozier sucked in a deep breath. His face held the suggestion of a hard smile.

"And you believe her?" he asked.

I said: "Absolutely."

Mick O'Rourke swore. He was staring at me with his mouth slightly opened.

Crozier turned toward the door of the suite. Near it he stopped and faced me again.

"You won't be disturbed if *I* do not feel as certain about Miss Vreedon as you?" he asked.

I said: "Yes, I'll be damned disturbed."

Crozier shrugged, smiling a little. "I'm sorry, Connors," he said. "But I've got a job to do."

I nodded. "I've got one to do, too," I replied. "It's to keep Sonia Vreedon from being dragged into a mess—when she doesn't belong in it."

Mick said: "What the hell, Al? You went and fell for—"

Crozier said calmly: "Babe Harron was dragged into the mess of death. It's not so bad when we're older. But he was just beginning to live—"

"So is the girl," I interrupted.

Crozier was silent for several seconds. Then he said very softly:

"Vennell first—he should be able to talk very soon. There are things for him to explain—important things."

I said: "Yes—damned important. But he may have been telling the truth—he may have been on the spot. And we might have the radiogram wrong. Or it might be a frameup—"

Crozier said: "Yes—it might be that. But when he talks—he can't afford to make mistakes."

Mick said slowly: "I don't think anyone in this tub—can afford to make mistakes, now."

Crozier looked at him with a peculiar expression in his eyes.

"You reason well, O'Rourke," he said. He smiled a little at me, went outside, closing the door after him. His footfalls died away along the corridor. Mick frowned at the door.

"That guy's shrewd," he said. His eyes went to mine. He spoke with a touch of grimness. "And you fell for Sonia Vreedon!"

I said: "Did I—or would it be nice to have one or two people *think* I've fallen for her?"

The big fellow said: "Jees, Al!"

He was thinking hard, his eyes almost closed. He said very slowly, after almost a minute:

"That guy's going to get something. He'll get it from Vennell—and it won't be long now!"

He swore softly. Then he turned his back and looked out of the port. When he faced me again, he said almost cheerfully:

"A lot of moon and stars—it's a swell night."

I looked at the door and thought suddenly about Griggs and the way he had glanced at the spot in the smoke room from which I had lifted the business card. Mick said again:

"It's warm and clear. Jees, what a night!"

I said grimly: "And so far as the *Virgin* is concerned, it's just about wasted."

Mick shrugged. "Well, we've got more guests than we started out with," he said.

I nodded. "And we'll go back with less than we started out with, maybe."

The big fellow yawned. "I don't feel right about taking that five grand from Vennell, Al."

I looked at his serious face. "Go along and hand it back," I suggested.

Mick shook his head. "He can't talk," he said.

I said: "What's his ability to talk got to do with it?"

The big fellow looked at me with narrowed eyes. He tapped a shoe against the suite floor.

"He'd want to thank me, wouldn't he?" he replied.

But he didn't smile as he said it.

·8·

TWELVE-THIRTY

THE way I felt, it was a little rough working up stuff for the chatter column. But I got enough done, and a pretty tight story of Babe Harron's collapse. I threw in a few sidelights and wrote some words to be tapped to Shaley, the city editor. But I left out a lot. It wasn't my job, anyway, and I knew that the papers would be smeared with the crew murder stuff. I found Risdon on deck and told him that I wanted to get the stuff over the wire to my paper. He grunted and said he's sent ashore Cy Dana's stuff an hour ago. I was slow.

I nodded. "It's the warm weather," I told him. "Couldn't be anything else—nothing ever happens around here."

He took my typewritten sheets and said he'd get them ashore and to the telegraph office. I asked him how Vennell was and he looked pretty grim.

"He's not talking yet," he said. "But Doctor Bryce says he'll be around pretty quick now. Shock, he says."

I nodded. Risdon said: "This fellow that flew up here from New York, the one Harron, senior, sent up, he's got a strong idea that the stroke was murdered in the boathouse—given the shot there. But he thinks the thing was handled from the yacht."

I said: "It sounds like the bunk to me."

Risdon smiled a little. "Everything sounds like the bunk to you, Connors—to your pal, O'Rourke, too."

I nodded. "We're just a couple of big cynics," I said. "Where's everybody?"

The lean-faced detective looked over the water of the Hudson, toward the new bridge.

"Most of 'em are in the big saloon, trying to be blasé as hell," he said grimly, and moved away from me.

I went inside and ran into Rita Velda. She looked tired.

"Where's everybody?" she asked me in a weary voice. "This is terrible."

I said: "Most of 'em are in the saloon, trying to be blasé as hell."

Her eyes widened a little. She went toward the big saloon. Near the smoke room I ran into Bryce. He was getting matches. I said:

"Is Vennell alone in his suite?"

Doctor Bryce shook his head. "Certainly not," he said sharply. "Crozier is with him just now."

I said: "Why *certainly* not?"

Bryce scowled beyond me. "Orders of his, and of Risdon's, that Eric isn't to be left alone."

I smiled a little. "Funny how well those two get along," I said. "In the books, when there are two dicks on a job—"

Bryce said: "Well, this isn't happening in a book, Connors. And Crozier isn't a dick. He's an investigator, and a friend of Babe Harron's father."

I nodded. "I still think it amounts to the same thing." I returned. "Crozier hasn't any more authority—"

The doctor interrupted again. "He's got more money behind him, and he's directly interested. Risdon has the police behind him—and they're working from the shore."

I said: "Vennell able to talk yet?"

Bryce shook his head. ''Shock,'' he muttered. ''Beats me—where he got to—or what happened. How he ever got back—''

He broke off, a puzzled expression on his face. He started for the door of the smoke room, but I stopped him.

''You've heard that the autopsy proved Harron had been morphined,'' I said. ''Could it work out that way?''

The doctor frowned at me. ''What way?'' he asked.

''If the Babe had been given the needle jab at the boathouse, say. How about the length of time it would take?''

Bryce looked at the floor. He spoke as though he were reciting.

''Morphine works through the system—the greater the resistance, the longer it takes. Harron was strong, in perfect shape. He was exerting himself. The exertion fought the poison. The murderer came very close to making the mistake of not administering the poison soon enough. There wasn't much delay at the start of this race.''

I said: ''As a doctor, how long would you say the poison took to work, in Harron's case?''

Bryce shrugged. ''It's very difficult to say,'' he stated. ''Doctor Vollmer thinks, from the size of the dose, that it was administered about forty minutes before Harron collapsed. It might have been thirty, or it might have been an hour.''

I said: ''Thanks—and how do you account for the fact that the Babe didn't feel the injection?''

Bryce smiled coldly. ''I don't account for it,'' he said. ''I know nothing of the facts—I'm a medical man. I do feel convinced that Harron died from the effects of a morphine injection. I think it was murder.''

He nodded his head and moved from the smoke room. I went over and sat down in a comfortable chair. I decided that things looked bad for Vennell. We could come pretty close to proving he had lied about his bets. And yet the next minute I wasn't so sure that we *could* come pretty close. There was the radiogram. But Vennell had stated that the apparatus hadn't been working. Captain Latham had backed him up. He could claim he knew nothing about the radiogram.

Babe Harron had been murdered, and California had lost a race in which they had been the favorite. They had been leading when Harron had collapsed. He was the stroke, the most important of the oarsmen. His failure would affect the crew more than the failure of any other man. The motive for murder pointed toward the loss of the race for California. It pointed in that direction from several angles, and yet it was not a surety. It required proof.

I thought of Vennell again. I wondered if he had other proof of the fact that he had been put on the spot, aside from the business card I had found and the entry of the masked man to his suite. I nodded my head almost unconsciously and decided that he probably had something that would serve as proof. Vennell was no fool. But, then, who had he turned away, when Columbia had won, staggering along the deck into the rain and darkness that had come with the storm? Was it because he had known that Babe Harron was dead? Was it because he had won a great sum of money—and that had been the reaction? Or were we wrong—and had he lost, after all?

I breathed to myself: "He was watching Sonia Vreedon so closely, before the race. I caught him at it several times. And Tim Burke swam out—talked with her—"

I broke off, got to my feet. It was growing late, but I did not think many of those aboard had turned in. I went from the smoke room and passed Cy Dana's cabin. He was shaving, with the door partly open. I said:

"Got a date, Cy?"

He swore at me. "Just good form," he replied. "Freshens my brain."

I said: "You flatter yourself," and went inside his cabin.

"Where's Torry Jones?" I asked. "I haven't seen him around much, though I hear he complained about Mick throwing him overboard."

Cy grinned. "He'll be around soon," he said. "It seems that Mick socked him in the jaw when he was dragging your intellectual down for the third time. Torry's giving the jaw the cold towel treatment, and it can't be done in public."

He put powder on his face and looked at me. He said: "It begins to look a little rough for our host, Al. When he starts to talk—"

He broke off. I nodded. "Venell's hard," I said. "It may take more than Poughkeepsie police and a private investigator to worry him. And he may not be mixed up in this, Cy."

Cy grunted. "Water may not be mixed up in Scotch," he said slowly, "but the chances are it is. The big thing is—who *else* is mixed up in this kill?"

I didn't say anything. Cy Dana said: "Vennell was on the yacht at about the time the masterminds are figuring Babe Harron was poisoned. We all saw him here—or most of us, anyway. Someone on the inside used the needle. Who?"

I didn't say anything to that, either. There were times when I liked to hear Cy talk. He had imagination. It was Cy who had tagged a wop named Mantilla the *Milan Mauler*. It developed later that Mantilla had never been any closer to Italy or Milan than Brooklyn.

Cy said: "There are a flock of rumors floating around the *Virgin*—"

I nodded. "There are always a flock of rumors floating around any virgin."

Cy frowned at me. "These are different," he said sternly. "Sonia Vreedon comes into this deal. And Mr. Timothy Burke."

I said: "That's rot."

He nodded. "Know anything about Burke?" he asked. "Has he got any money? Wouldn't he like to have some? It might take a little to do the right thing by Sonia Vreedon. Accustomed as she is to the better things in life—"

I groaned. "With your imagination—you should write a novel, Cy."

He nodded. "I can't punctuate," he replied.

I said: "How about the publishers?"

He shook his head. "They can't either," he replied. "So that's out."

I leaned against the wall of his cabin and half closed my eyes. Cy said:

"How's that palooka of yours going to come out, when this gets real messy?"

I looked serious. "You refer to Mr. O'Rourke?" I said coldly.

He nodded. "Yeah—the guy that nearly killed Dingo Bandelli with his bare fists. The guy that was Andy Dormer's bodyguard for a while, until Andy got economic."

I stood up straight and smiled at Cy. He smiled back at me and started to tie his tie.

"So you knew that—all along," I said softly.

He nodded. "Sure, but I believed you when you said he was a funny guy, Al. I always believe you."

I swore at him. "That's one thing about this yacht," I said. "Everyone is so trusting. Everyone believes everyone else."

He nodded. "Just a big happy family. *Eric Vennell and His Friends on the Hudson, or Al and Mick at the Regatta*."

His voice held sarcasm. I said: "Well, Vennell called me up and said he had a three or four day job for a guy that was tough and could shoot. He said he wouldn't have to do either, he didn't think. Mick wasn't exactly busy, so I got him. He'd never seen a regatta."

Cy nodded. "And when he gets through with this one, he may not want to see another for a long, long time!" he said grimly.

2

There were a lot of people in the saloon. The blonde who had been so shocked when Hunch had brought Mick and me aboard and had used a bad word—she was talking with the dignified-looking gentleman who had felt that the yacht burned crude oil. Torry Jones sat in a corner, with his back turned to most of the room. Don Rayne was talking with a man named Burns, and Rita Velda tapped cigarette ashes into a tray near the center table. The gray-haired woman said in her too loud voice:

"It is growing steadily warmer."

Rita tapped her straight, reddish hair and smiled wearily. I watched a short, chunky girl who it seemed to me had been referred to as "Bubbles," as she moved toward the cabinet radio. Someone said: "Please don't, Miss Lacey." She sighed and went toward Torry Jones.

Carla Sard was sitting near the center table, reading. I looked around the room several times before I discovered Sonia. She was seated in a low chair that had been placed in a sort of alcove spot. Risdon was seated close to her and they were talking in low tones.

I went over near Carla and looked at the cover of the magazine which she was reading. It looked literary—and a little analytical. There were high-sounding titles and foreign-sounding names on the cover. I said:

"Anything of Balzac's in that issue, Miss Sard?"

Rita Velda laughed nastily, and Carla's body stiffened. She flashed me one of her Hollywood smiles, and it wasn't at all bad.

"I don't think she has anything in this magazine," she said cheerfully.

I wasn't quite sure who was kidding whom. Rita said, without looking at either of us:

"How about George Sand—has *he* got anything in it?"

Carla ignored the other woman. She toned her smile down so that it didn't include her teeth.

"You mean the Balzac who wrote *Lost Ladies*, don't you, Mr. Connors?" she asked.

I still wasn't sure about things. Rita said:

"That was William Cather, Carla."

Carla slammed the magazine shut, and tossed it aside. Rita smiled at me and moved away. I said:

"Take it easy, Carla—don't start anything. Vennell's cabin isn't so far from the saloon."

She muttered fiercely: "I hate that woman, Al!"

I smiled and went over to pick up the magazine. She said:

"Let it lay, Al."

I let it lay. "Don't you want to finish the story?" I asked.

She shook her head. "I was damn near asleep anyway," she replied. "It's lousy."

I shrugged and moved toward a chair that was not far from the ones occupied by Sonia and Risdon. Risdon was doing most of the talking, and Sonia seemed to be shaking her head a great deal. I couldn't catch any words.

After a few minutes one of the deck doors opened and Captain Latham came in. He looked pretty snappy in his white uniform, but his face held a serious expression. He looked around, and then went directly to Risdon's side. I heard the names "Vollmer" and "Mears." And then the captain looked sharply at Sonia. He said something else, and I caught the name "Burke."

Sonia Vreedon's body jerked a little; she half rose from her chair. But she relaxed. She touched her lips with a small handkerchief, and she acted pretty nervous.

Risdon spoke to her, stood up, and bowed a little. He smiled at her. Then he followed Captain Latham from the saloon to the port-side deck.

I waited a few seconds, rose, and went over beside Sonia. She smiled at me, but there were tears in her eyes.

"What's up now?" I asked.

She spoke very softly. "The California coach, Mears—and Tim Burke have come out," she said. "And the crew doctor, Vollmer."

I frowned at the floor. "What for?" I murmured.

She looked somewhere beyond me. "More questioning, I suppose," she said. "Poor Tim!"

I looked at the wall clock, at one end of the saloon. It was almost twelve-thirty.

"It's a strange hour for them to come out here," I said. "Must be something important."

Sonia was trying to fight back the tears. I leaned forward.

"Somehow," I said. "I don't think Tim Burke is mixed up in this. I know you're not. But if there's something—something that makes it seem tough, Sonia—"

She shook her head. I said: "I wish you'd tell me. I may be able to help."

She got to her feet, and so did I. She said in a shaken voice:

"I'm going—to my cabin. If they want me—"

I nodded and stood aside. "Get some sleep," I advised. "This'll be all right—"

She said indignantly: "Sleep! As though I could sleep!"

She moved away. I watched Don Rayne open the door for her—one that opened to a corridor running forward to the cabins. I stood for a little while, thinking. Doctor Bryce came into the room, using the same doorway through which Sonia had passed. Rayne asked him a question and he shook his head. He looked around the room.

I looked around, too, wondering where Mick O'Rourke was. Bryce saw me and came across the room. He reached my side.

"Where's Risdon?" he asked.

I told him I thought the detective was on deck, with the crew coach and doctor and Tim Burke. I rather expected him to be surprised, but he wasn't.

"Eric's out of it," he said. "He can talk now and knows what he's saying. But they've got to go easy with him. Crozier seems to realize that—he's waiting and just humoring him. But I've got to make Risdon understand. He's a more aggressive type."

I nodded. Risdon came back into the saloon from the port side of the deck, and Bryce waved a hand to him. The detective came over to us.

Bryce said: "Vennell's conscious. But you've got to go very easy. If you want to ask questions, keep your voice low. He's still suffering from shock."

Risdon nodded. His greenish eyes met mine. He said very softly:

"I've got questions to ask, all right. The coach found the hypodermic needle that was used on Babe Harron."

Bryce uttered a little exclamation. I stared at Risdon. Bryce said:

"Where?"

Risdon's voice was almost a whisper. He looked at me as he spoke.

"In the mattress of the cot occupied by Tim Burke," he said.

Bryce drew a quick breath. I didn't say anything. Thoughts of Sonia were rushing through my head. Bryce said slowly:

"Good God—in *Burke's* mattress!"

Risdon nodded. "It looks as though we're getting at—"

His words died away as the lights in the saloon dimmed. They went down slowly; there were cries of surprise and a few squeals of nervous laughter. Then they flared again. Almost instantly there was the sound of a shot.

It came from some spot forward, so far as I could judge. It was faint, but not faint enough to be on the shore. And then, from some spot much nearer, there came the sharper sound of a second shot!

There was a cry from the corridor beyond the saloon—the voice of Crozier sounded.

"Risdon—what's wrong?"

The lights started to dim again. They got very low, came up a little—and then we were in blackness. And there was no light from the decks, or from any other part of the *Virgin*.

There was the sound of footfalls, rapid ones. Crozier's voice reached us again, near the saloon. He called out:

"Who fired that shot?"

There was confusion in the saloon. I heard Risdon move away from me, saying sharply:

"The rest of you—stay where you are!"

And then there was the voice of Vennell. It reached us in a sort of half-scream. It was filled with fear, distorted.

"O'Rourke—Connors—for God's sake—"

Risdon was trying to get to the door that led to the corridor. He was stumbling. Carla Sard screamed shrilly. Crozier's voice came into the room.

"Vennell's—cabin!"

There was a crashing sound in the corridor, and Captain Latham's voice reached me from the port-side deck.

"Get those—lights on!"

But there was no light. Above the sounds of confusion in the saloon I heard the hoarse voice of Mick O'Rourke. It sounded as though it came from some spot forward of even Vennell's suite. He called out:

"I'm coming—Vennell—"

I thought of Sonia Vreedon. She had left the saloon. Mick O'Rourke had not been in the room. Crozier was outside, but near the door. The thoughts ran through my head as Bryce brushed me aside and got moving. Someone struck a match as we headed for the corridor.

The lights did not come on. There was the beam of a flashlight down the corridor a short distance. Beyond the passageway that led off a wider one to the spot at which Vennell's cabin was located, the beam struck the huge figure of Mick O'Rourke. He was moving swiftly forward.

The flash was in the hands of Crozier; he turned into the passage that led to Vennell's suite. Mick was behind him. Bryce was just ahead of me as we made the turn.

The yacht was still in darkness. I had the feeling that every light was off, that not one bulb on the *Virgin* held power. Bryce pulled up short, behind the big figure of Mick, who stood in the doorway of Vennell's suite.

Crozier's voice reached us, from within the cabin.

"Vennell—Vennell—who did it?"

Mick O'Rourke moved inside. Bryce and I followed. Vennell was on the floor. He was propped up, so that his head rested against one of the wicker chairs. His hands were at his sides, hanging limply. His eyes were wide—and staring straight ahead. There was a twisted smile on his lips, at once grotesque and terrible.

Bryce leaned forward and touched a wrist. After a few seconds he said very slowly:

"He's—dead."

Mick O'Rourke swore. Crozier stood up, but kept the light on Vennell's body. Doctor Bryce continued to lean forward. He said unsteadily:

"It's the back of his head—crushed. All smashed in."

Crozier said: "He hasn't been shot?"

There was a little silence, then Bryce said:

"Not shot—it's the back of his head. He's been hit a terrible blow—"

Crozier moved the beam of his flash around the suite. There was nothing upset. Not a chair was overturned. There was no sign of disorder. The sheets on Vennell's bed were thrown aside, that was all.

Bryce said slowly: "He had just—regained consciousness. He could talk—"

I said: "There were shots—who fired them?"

Crozier didn't seem to hear me. He muttered:

"Well—he can't talk—*now*."

There was silence, except for sounds beyond the corridor, and Captain Latham's voice calling sharply for the second officer.

The beam of Crozier's flash struck our faces, one by one. We all looked pretty grim. But I didn't see Risdon. He had been the first to make a break for the corridor. He wasn't in the suite now.

Crozier lowered the beam so that it struck Vennell's body again. Mick said hoarsely:

"Jees—they got him, Al!"

No one spoke. A bell struck, somewhere forward, and another one struck, aft. Bryce said very softly:

"Twelve-thirty."

Torry Jones voice came to us, from the passageway beyond the suite.

"What happened—is Vennell all right?"

Crozier looked at Mick. He said very steadily:

Go out and tell them, O'Rourke."

Mick said huskily: "What'll I tell 'em?"

Crozier let his flash beam move around the suite again. When he spoke, his tone was almost casual.

"Tell them all we know, O'Rourke—and that's that Eric Vennell is dead."

·9·

THE FOURTH REASON

It was almost two o'clock in the morning when I went on deck for some air. The yacht was lighted pretty brightly; there were several launches along side. A uniformed police officer strolled along the starboard deck stretch and looked at me suspiciously as I stopped and used cupped hands to light a cigarette. I said:

"I'm Connors—newspaperman. Just up for a bit of air. Not going anywhere."

He had a round face, very brown. He said in a grim tone:

"I guess that's true enough."

I went aft and ran into Cy Dana leaning against a rail and looking up at the stars. The night was pretty hot; there was no breeze. Cy nodded to me.

"You've got nerve, Al," he said.

"In which way?" I asked.

He shrugged. "You're still bunking with that guy O'Rourke," he said.

I nodded. "Why not?"

Cy frowned. "He's a killer, Al," he said. "You know that, and I think Crozier knows it. And Risdon, too."

I pulled up a wicker deck chair. We were alone aft, but the uniformed officer was along the deck stretch, looking out over the water and twisting his head toward us every few seconds. I sat in the chair and spoke in a low tone.

"He's killed, if that's what you mean," I agreed. "But I know a lot of good chaps that have killed—and that got paid for it. And that got medals for it."

Cy Dana swore at me. "The guy that morphined Babe Harron won't get medals," he said. "And the one who battered Vennell's head in—he won't get any. This isn't a war."

I looked at Dana for several seconds without saying anything. Then I said quietly:

"Got any ideas, Cy?"

He nodded. "A lot of 'em," he replied. "You'll think they're all rotten, too."

I said: "Probably. One of them is that Tim Burke morphined Babe Harron. I could see that, by the expression on your face when Crozier was questioning him."

Cy shrugged. "It doesn't look so good for Burke," he said. "He had the opportunity to use the needle. The needle was found in his cot mattress. He probably didn't figure anyone would take the trouble to go through mattresses. This fellow Mears is pretty thorough."

I grunted. "If I'd used morphine on a man, and got the idea of a mattress hide for the needle, I wouldn't use my *own* mattress," I said.

Cy Dana said grimly: "You might not have had time to use any other one, or the opportunity."

I said: "All right. Burke morphined Babe Harron and got rid of the needle he had swiped from the crew doctor, Vollmer. What was his reason?"

Cy Dana said slowly: "Nine times out of ten there are just two motives for murder—greed and revenge. I don't know much about Burke. There might be some reason for revenge, though Mears doesn't know of any. And he thinks he would know. Crew is a closely knit affair. The coach is right with the men, and the men have to be right together. Burke, then, didn't hate Harron. Nor was he his particular pal. Mears says Burke was quiet and as much alone as any crew man could be. We'll throw out the revenge idea—and call it greed."

I said: "What sort of greed?"

Cy smiled a little. "The most obvious sort—money greed. Burke hasn't any money—he's working his way through California. This was his last race, too. And he hasn't any business prospects, he admits that. And he is pretty crazy about Sonia Vreedon. She's a lawyer's daughter, but he didn't take law. She's an expensive girl to marry."

I said: "How do you know?"

Cy shrugged. "She's always had money," he replied.

I groaned. "All right, go ahead," I said. "Use your imagination, Cy."

He smiled a little grimly. "I'm giving you a possible theory, backed up by certain facts," he stated. "There was a chance for Burke to make a lot of money. He had only to do two things—get the hypodermic syringe from Vollmer's kit and use it. He had advice."

I said: "He had to get the morphine—and fill the syringe. He had to use it in a way that Babe Harron didn't know what had happened. You think that was simple?"

Cy Dana frowned. "That's the thing that beats me," he said. "How was it that the stroke didn't know there had been an injection? That's tough."

I smiled grimly. "Well—we'll let that pass. You say Burke had advice. Who gave it to him?"

The sportswriter looked past me. "Why not Mick O'Rourke?" he said softly.

I sat up straight in the deck chair. I stared at Cy.

"What the devil are you getting at?" I breathed "Mick O'Rourke!"

Cy nodded. ''I said why not Mick O'Rourke,'' he reminded. ''It's a theory—not a fact. Something went wrong. Tim didn't just swim out here to see Sonia Vreedon. That's silly, and you know it. He's got strong character—he'll talk just so much, no more. Risdon and Crozier have been shooting questions at him for an hour, but he keeps repeating the same thing. He's no fool. And only a fool would have made that swim to see a girl that he could have seen the next day, after the race. Mears has told me, as a matter of fact, that Burke could have seen her at the boathouse, before the race. The coach wanted the crew in the best mood. If it would have helped Tim any—to see the girl—it could have been arranged.''

I half closed my eyes. ''I supposed she handed Tim the information he needed,'' I said slowly.

Cy waited a few seconds. ''Or the morphine he needed,'' he said in a hard voice.

I rose and stood close to him. He looked at me and smiled a little.

''Keep cool, Al,'' he advised. ''I'm giving you a theory. You asked for it.''

I said: ''That's the damnedest thing I've ever heard you say—Sonia passing the morphine—''

Cy said: ''She didn't go to see him before the race. Why not? Other people went to the boathouse. I did, for one. Don Rayne did. But Sonia Vreedon stayed away. Why?''

I shrugged. ''There might be a dozen reasons,'' I said. ''Well—why did she stay away?''

Cy Dana lighted a cigarette. ''Because she knew Babe Harron was going to be morphined,'' he said slowly. ''And she didn't want any established evidence of a meeting with Tim Burke. She thought something might go wrong. She's a pretty keen girl—the daughter of a criminal lawyer. She tried to play safe.''

I said: ''Oh, God!''

Cy looked at the glowing tip of his cigarette.

"But you saw Burke out here—and you talked to Risdon. And Johnny Light, the Number Two oar, he spotted Burke at the boathouse end. And Sonia Vreedon now admits that she talked with him at the yacht. She was just up getting air, because she was excited and couldn't sleep. Can you imagine Sonia Vreedon getting so excited she couldn't sleep—over a crew race?"

I couldn't, but I said that I could. Cy just shrugged.

"Knowing what was going to happen before the race, she might have been excited," he said. "But that wasn't the reason she was on deck. She expected Burke."

I sighed. "You figure Tim was advised by O'Rourke," I said. "Why didn't Mick meet him, then?"

Cy said: "Because you were sleeping in the same cabin with him. He had to be careful."

I groaned again. "And who was Mick working for?" I asked sarcastically. "Vennell?"

Cy nodded. "Of course," he said. "Vennell cleaned up when Columbia won, but he had to be *sure* that Columbia would win. He used O'Rourke and Sonia Vreedon—and Burke. And he cleaned up."

I moved round a little and finally came back close to Cy.

"It's the most hellish theory I ever heard," I said. "It sounds like a bum sort of joke to me."

Cy said grimly: "Yeah—we'll start to shoot it full of holes, Al. And lay a bet that it isn't the theory that Risdon and Crozier will follow to the finish."

I swore and looked toward the Highland shore. There were few lights showing in the houses on the hill that rose in back of the small town.

Cy Dana said: "The police are holding the California crew in the boathouse, and they're working on shore as well as the yacht. Harron, senior, has plenty of money. They'll get his son's murderer—and the others involved."

I nodded. "I hope so. But it won't be Sonia Vreedon, or Mick O'Rourke," I said.

Cy didn't reply. He kept his eyes narrowed on mine.

"For a newspaperman—you're going all haywire, Al," he said.

I nodded. "All right—Vennell worked Mick O'Rourke, Sonia, and Tim Burke to murder the stroke so that California would lose, Columbia won, and he cleaned up, we'll say. Now, first, *I* got Mick O'Rourke aboard. How about that?"

Cy smiled. "You didn't have any trouble locating O'Rourke, did you?" he asked. "After Vennell told you his troubles?"

I shook my head. "Not much," I said.

Cy Dana nodded. "Vennell figured you'd get O'Rourke. But if you hadn't he would have got him aboard some other way. It was better to have you bring him aboard, with that sloppy story of yours. He had to give you a reason, so he worked the on-the-spot gag. O'Rourke played along—he's still playing along. And if you don't watch yourself—"

I said: "Bunk."

Cy nodded. "I'm older than you, Al," he said. "I don't fall in love so easily."

I swore at him. "How about Vennell?" I asked in a low tone.

Cy turned his head and looked at the uniformed officer up the deck some distance.

"Figure it out for yourself," he said. "I'll pass up what happened when Vennell disappeared, right after the finish. He'd won a lot of money, and he knew it. Maybe something snapped, inside of his head. I think he went overboard. Maybe he was knocked over—or maybe he just lost his head. He'd been under tremendous strain. He'd had a few minutes there when it hadn't looked as though the job had been done right. Columbia was being licked. Anyway, he got back aboard again."

I said with sarcasm: "After almost four hours of floating round in the Hudson."

Cy shrugged. "He might not have floated round in the Hudson. Captain Latham says he was a strong swimmer. He might easily have reached shore. The storm was on—and he might easily not have been seen. Then he got back."

I said: "With a pretty badly cut head."

Cy skipped his cigarette overboard. "Not badly enough to keep him unconscious so long, unless I'm all wrong," he replied. "Shock might have done that—and then, again, it might not. Anyway, he was back aboard the yacht, and two detectives were aboard. One of them knew that the yacht was the right working spot—he was working pretty fast. Burke had given him the lead. And Vennell was at a point where he would have had to talk pretty quick."

The sportswriter paused. I said: "Someone threw the main light switch—there were a lot of shots—and someone murdered Vennell."

Cy nodded. "Someone who was pretty damn strong." he said very quietly. "Someone who hadn't been in the main saloon when the lights went out."

I kicked the wicker chair around but I didn't sit in it.

"There were quite a few people aboard who were not in the main saloon," I said.

He nodded. "Yeah. Sonia Vreedon and Mick O'Rourke—"

He let his voice die. He lighted another cigarette. I said slowly:

"One of them murdered Vennell, because they were afraid he was breaking down and might talk. That would have involved them."

Cy said: "I don't think Sonia Vreedon did it, Al."

I groaned. "You should have been a dick, Cy," I told him "You're damn good."

The sportswriter nodded. "I've got three theories," he said. "The one I've told you is about the sanest."

I shook my head. "It's lousy," I said. "And you know it."

Cy said: "It's pretty damn good, Al. Here and there it's shaky. But it isn't lousy. And you know that."

We were both silent for several minutes. Then I said:

"Well, Crozier tells me the yacht stays anchored until they get something. Risdon says the same thing. They're going to hold the crew together, and it looks as though Coach Mears, Doc Vollmer, and Tim Burke will stay aboard tonight. Vennell's dead, but—"

Cy nodded. "But Tim Burke might talk, under certain conditions." he stated. "Or Sonia Vreedon might talk. Or Mick O'Rourke might—"

I reached for my cigarettes, shaking my head. A figure came along the deck, said something to the uniformed officer, and moved on toward us. Cy said:

"Risdon."

The lean-faced Poughkeepsie detective came up to us and looked into our faces sharply. His own eyes were serious.

"You fellows trying to put anything over on me?" he asked grimly.

I watched Cy Dana look hurt. He shook his head.

"What could we put over, Risdon?" I asked.

He smiled a little. "I mean—are you figuring on sending stuff ashore, for your sheets?"

I had stuff in my pocket that I was figuring doing just that with, and I guessed that Cy had, too. He nodded his head.

"We ought to get in a flash on the Vennell murder," he said. "It's a big story—he's well known."

Risdon said: "Let me read the stuff first."

Cy Dana and I exchanged glances. The lean-faced detective shrugged.

"If you don't it won't get ashore," he said simply. "All I want to see is that you don't give someone a break."

I frowned at him. "My story simply tells who was where when the murder was committed and doesn't do any guessing."

Risdon smiled grimly. "Yes?" he said. "Well, where were O'Rourke, Miss Vreedon, Captain Latham, Doctor Vollmer, Tim Burke, the second officer, most of the crew, and a few others?"

Cy said: "Ah—you see, Al? You forgot something."

Risdon scowled at Cy. I said: "Haven't they told you where they were, Risdon?"

He nodded, his face grim. "Sure," he said. "They were all quite busy doing very splendid things, far from Vennell's suite."

I took some sheets of paper from a pocket and handed them to him.

"Here's my stuff," I said. "I've given you a nice boost too."

Risdon took the paper. "Thanks," he said with sarcasm. "But I wouldn't take charge of the New York police force if I got the offer. Poughkeepsie suits me."

Cy said: "It must be quiet and everything."

The lean-faced detective nodded. "Except when the Vassar girls break out the daisy chain," he said.

Cy handed him a few sheets of paper. Risdon stuffed them in his pocket.

"I'll look them right over—and send them ashore if they're all right." he said. "I don't like to hold up the press."

Cy said: "It's getting late—and I haven't been a reporter for so long the city desk will have to rewrite my stuff. I want to make the morning edition."

I nodded. "Don't mix the two up. It'll be a tough break for me," I said to Risdon.

Cy smiled faintly. Risdon said: "It doesn't look too good for young Tim Burke, but I don't want it spread all over the papers."

I looked toward Highland and the few lights that showed

in houses. There were some showing in the California boathouse, too. I said:

"Tim Burke didn't use the hypodermic on babe Harron, Risdon."

The greenish eyes of the detective were narrowed on mine.

"No?" he asked. "Well, who did?"

I shook my head. "Someone who was pretty desperate," I replied. "Tim Burke wasn't desperate. He may not have had any brilliant business prospects, or much money in sight. But he's young—and strong. He's not the type to kill this way. He hasn't been disillusioned enough."

Cy Dana groaned. Risdon said: "How do you know he wasn't desperate? How do you know he wasn't disillusioned?"

I said: "Was he?"

Risdon swore softly. "You newspaper guys think you're second Christs," he breathed.

Cy Dana said: "Damned if they don't, Risdon."

The detective turned away from us and walked toward the main saloon. I called after him:

"Find out who pulled the master switch?"

He shook his head. "That would help a lot, wouldn't it?" he called back with sarcasm.

He went inside, slamming the door that led from the deck. Cy Dana said:

"Risdon's a little suspicious of everybody."

I nodded. "Why not? He's established the fact that Vennell made a big gambling win. And when he figured he'd have money to pass around later—he might have passed it before. Risdon doesn't know who might have got it."

Cy Dana nodded his head slowly: "I didn't know you were willing to admit that Risdon had established the fact Vennell cleaned up on Columbia."

I shrugged. "I gave Crozier the radiogram I'd found.

He's talked with Sonia, and she sensed that Vennell was betting against California. She's probably told Crozier that. I don't think he's holding much back from Risdon."

Cy said: "That doesn't establish the fact that Vennell bet against California."

A door opened, up the deck a short distance. A head stuck out and Crozier called:

"Oh, Connors!"

I said: "Here."

Crozier stepped outside, and then stood still. He called softly:

"Come inside a few minutes, will you? Want to talk to you."

I said: "Sure."

Cy Dana sighed. "Better be good, Al." he advised. "A hunk of lead pipe hurts like the devil."

"Crozier isn't that sort of a dick," I replied. "He's an investigator, Cy."

The sportswriter nodded. "Yeah," he said tightly. "But when a guy's after a murderer, he forgets a lot of the sophisticated stuff, except in books."

"If I get hurt, my sheet'll sue," I announced cheerfully.

The sportswriter grunted. "Sue 'em for not killing you!" he muttered.

2

Crozier led the way to the captain's quarters. Captain Latham was not inside the well-done living room of his suite, but Sonia Vreedon sat in a high-backed chair, facing one that was not so comfortable and that had cigarette ashes on the cushion. Crozier gestured toward a third chair, near the one in which Sonia was seated.

I smiled at her, and she smiled back. It seemed to me that she had been crying, but that she'd got past that stage. There was something that looked a little like defiance in her gray eyes. He slender body was relaxed in the chair; she held a cigarette in her left-hand fingers.

I took the chair near her and lighted up. Crozier sat down in the one that faced Sonia's, ran fingers through his gray hair, and tapped his mustache a few times. His pale-blue eyes seemed almost cheerful.

"We go along this way, Connors," he said thoughtfully, and stopped speaking for several seconds. "We reach the conclusion that, having lost a great deal of money on Wall Street, Vennell decided on a rather desperate scheme for getting it back. He had a large sum left—say, three quarters of a million. He distributed that sum over the country, taking the short end of a three-to-one bet. He realized that while there was always betting on crew races, there has never been what might be called organized betting. But he was betting against the favorite crew—a veteran crew. So he could not simply bet. He was a gambler, and a shady one. We know that. He had to be sure that California would lose the race, and yet he had to be sure that the crew was a favorite until he got his money out and covered. The radiogram proves that he got it covered."

I said: "If the radiogram wasn't a fake."

Crozier smiled faintly. "It wasn't," he said. "I've been after the radio operator. There has been nothing the matter with the apparatus, as was reported. Vennell simply didn't want interference. It took some digging to get the truth, but, with Vennell dead, things are different. Some of the people aboard are getting worried."

I whistled softly. Crozier said: "And some of them aren't."

His eyes went to the gray ones of Sonia Vreedon. She didn't say anything. I said:

"Perhaps they have nothing to be worried about."

Crozier tapped his mustache. "Perhaps not," he agreed, but his voice was grim. "In any case, Vennell got his money covered. It might not have been so much as I suggest. But I'd gamble that it was in excess of a half-million."

He paused and frowned. "Vennell was pretty shrewd," he went on. "He was trying to put over a big thing, and his nerves were none too good. He knew that. He had something to beat—himself. He was pretty sure he'd go to pieces during the race, except for one thing. And he wanted to cover up anything that might show. His own nervousness, his own strange actions. So he called you on the phone and got you to bring along a bodyguard. He knew pretty well who you'd bring."

I said: "I don't think he did. And what do you mean—he was pretty sure he'd go to pieces, except for one thing?"

Crozier said quietly: "He was using stuff."

I stared at him. My eyes went to Sonia; she was tapping ash from her cigarette. Her own eyes were expressionless.

I said: "Stuff, eh? What sort?"

Crozier leaned back in his chair. "Morphine," he said quietly.

There was a little silence. Then the investigator said slowly:

"He knew it might show—there might be a letdown. So he decided upon the story that he had been put on the spot by a big shot whose money a brokerage house with which he was connected had refused to return, after a natural loss on the market. And because he didn't want to appear to be hiding anything, he invited a mixed crowd, including two newspaper men. The only thing he stressed, to two of you—O'Rourke and yourself—was that his life was in danger. He told you he had a small bet, for him, on California."

I narrowed my eyes and nodded my head a little. Crozier was talking pretty straight. I waited. The gray-haired investigator said:

"He wanted to be convincing—so that if he went to

pieces, you wouldn't associate it with his real activities, but with this threat on his life. So he planted that business card you found, in the smoke room. Or, rather, he had someone else plant it."

I sucked in a sharp breath. "Griggs?" I breathed questioningly.

Sonia looked at me sharply, and I thought there was sudden fear in her eyes. Crozier looked surprised. He leaned forward in his chair.

"How'd you know that?" he snapped.

I shrugged, smiling. "After I'd picked the card up and put it in my pocket, Griggs came into the smoke room to do something. He looked down at the spot from which I'd lifted the card."

Sonia was breathing quickly; she leaned back and closed her eyes now. Crozier nodded.

"Griggs was very much an amateur, of course. I went after him, showed him the card. He denied knowledge of it, at first. But he changed his mind, after Vennell was murdered. He came to me and told me the truth. He didn't want to be involved in something serious. Vennell had instructed him to drop the card and to be silent about it. He had told Griggs it was a joke. I don't know whose handwriting it was. The intent was merely to build up his story that his life was in danger."

I frowned. "And the one who got into his cabin?"

Crozier said slowly: "It's a thin story—that one. I haven't had time to talk with Carla Sard yet. But when I do, it may fall to pieces. That was a little stupid of Vennell, but he might have conceived that at a time when he wasn't thinking too clearly and was obsessed with the idea that he must impress the fact that his life really was in danger."

I said nothing. Sonia was breathing more easily now, her head tilted back slightly and her eyes looking toward the ceiling of the living room.

Crozier said: ''Well—that gets us along a bit. Babe Harron was the stroke of the California crew. Important, very. If he went to pieces, there was much more chance of the others going to pieces. So Vennell decided he was the one to go to pieces.''

I said: ''Cold-blooded murder.''

Crozier shook his head. ''I don't think so,'' he said quietly. ''Something went wrong. There was a mistake or something got away from Vennell.''

He paused and lighted a cigarette. I looked at Sonia and said:

''You mean—someone saw a chance to cut in?''

Crozier shrugged. ''Miss Vreedon doesn't think so,'' he replied grimly.

Sonia spoke for the first time. She said in a husky but steady voice:

''Crozier and this man Risdon—they both think that poor Tim injected the morphine—''

Her voice broke. She stood up suddenly and turned her back to both of us. Her hands were clenched at her sides. I said:

''You're wrong, Crozier—Tim Burke isn't mixed up in this.''

The investigator smiled with his lips. ''In the shell he was directly in front of Babe Harron—that is, ahead of him,'' he said. ''In the boathouse quarters he had his cot next to Harron's.''

I said: ''What of that?''

''He had the better opportunity,'' Crozier replied quietly.

Sonia Vreedon swung around suddenly. She faced the investigator from New York. She said in a level voice:

''He didn't do it, I tell you. He didn't. He couldn't.''

Crozier spread his hands in a swift gesture, palms up, then let them fall to his knees.

''That isn't good enough, Miss Vreedon. He's obstinate. He won't answer all questions—only the ones he wishes to answer. The hypodermic syringe was found in the mattress of his cot—''

I said slowly: ''How did Coach Mears happen to get the idea of a mattress search?''

Crozier shook his head. ''He didn't get the idea,'' he replied. ''I got it.''

I said: ''Pardon.''

He nodded.

Sonia repeated slowly: ''Tim didn't do it—it's ghastly, just to think he did.''

I looked at Crozier, who seemed grimly amused.

''If the injection had been made in the boathouse, Babe Harron would have known it,'' I said evenly. ''He would have had time to find out what had happened. A clever man would have realized that. If the injection had been made while the shell was being pulled in leisurely fashion, up the river, for the start, things would have been different. There wouldn't have been time for an examination. Tim Burke's face was to Harron's back. Harron was a big man, broad-shouldered, powerful, naturally. Burke might have leaned forward, Ed Dale, the coxswain, was facing him, but he would not have seen a swift movement. Number Six might have been looking behind or fooling with his slide rig. The paddle out for the start can be haphazard affair. There is certainly a possibility that the injection might have been made in the shell.''

Sonia's hurt eyes were on mine. Crozier had his narrowed; he nodded his head.

I said: ''Supposing the injection was made—the time limit is still right, for the poison. Supposing Babe Harron feels the sharp sting of the needle—''

Sonia said: ''Please! I can't—''

She moved toward a port. I said: ''I'm sorry, but this is a point, Sonia. A big one.''

Crozier kept narrowed eyes on mine. ''Go ahead,'' he said grimly.

"Harron feels the sting—he turns," I said quietly.

"Tim Burke says: 'That damn bee!'—or something of the sort. A bee can get quite a distance from shore. Or a fly—a big one. Harron believes Burke, of course. And what can he do about it? It's too late for treatment, and an insect sting isn't going to stop Harron from stroking. He knows that. It may hurt—it's a tough break—but it isn't going to check him any. He swears a few times, and the crew rows on up for the start."

Crozier said: "It's a damn sweet possibility."

Sonia shook her head. "No—no!" she cried, her voice rising. "You know that isn't what happened! You know it!"

I looked at Crozier. "You admit that it could have happened that way—and that the chances were better in the shell—better because Babe didn't have time to examine his shoulder? It's an awkward spot to get at—the left shoulder blade."

The investigator nodded slowly, his eyes slitted on mine.

"The shell was a better spot," he said very quietly.

I smiled at him. "Then why was the hypodermic needle found in Tim Burke's mattress?" I asked. "Certainly he would have dropped it over the side of the shell."

Sonia swung around, her eyes suddenly wide. She said: "If Tim *had* done it—that way—of course he would have dropped it overboard."

Crozier smiled at me. "You were using your head, Connors," he said quietly. "You've trapped me into admitting something in Burke's favor, eh?"

I nodded. "I hope so," I said. "My point is that the shell was the best spot for the injection—and yet Tim Burke didn't do it. If he had, he wouldn't have held on to the needle."

Sonia said: "Yes—yes—can't you see? He's told you he doesn't know a thing—"

Crozier kept his eyes on mine. "There are two points,

Connors. Burke might not have been able to get rid of the syringe. He might have shoved it down under his trunks again. That's one. The other is that in spite of the fact that the shell appears to have been the better spot for the injection—it wasn't made there."

I said grimly: "I can't imagine the injection having been made in the boathouse."

Crozier was silent for several seconds. then he spoke softly:

"But you've got to admit that there would be hardly any other crew man in a position to make the injection in the shell."

I frowned. Sonia said unsteadily:

"But you know Tim wouldn't have taken the syringe back to the boathouse and put it in his mattress. You know he would have had some opportunity to get it into the water!"

I nodded. "He certainly would have," I said. "With that storm sweeping the river, at the finish—all that confusion."

Crozier pulled on his cigarette. "Then I think that in spite of the fact that the shell offered the best opportunity, the injection wasn't made there."

I shook my head slowly. "You're pretty convinced that Tim Burke was Vennell's accomplice. Why, aside from the evidence of the syringe found in his mattress?"

The gray-haired investigator nodded his head. He looked somewhere beyond me.

"Why did Burke swim out here—the night before the race?" he said. "I'm not satisfied with his explanation. Nor Miss Vreedon's."

I looked at Sonia. "What is the explanation?" I asked.

Crozier remained silent, and Sonia spoke in a low, husky tone.

"Tim was foolish, that's all. He wanted to see me. I happened to be on deck."

Crozier exchanged glances with me. I said as gently as I could:

"Did a few hours make so much difference? Couldn't he have waited until morning?"

There was scorn in Sonia's dark eyes. She said:

"Can *you* look back and say that everything you've done has been wise? I have said he was foolish. But—just the same—"

She checked herself. There wasn't any doubt that she loved Tim Burke. I could see it in her eyes, and feel it in her words—sense it in the ones she left unsaid. She turned away from us again, moving toward a port.

Crozier said wearily: "I'm tired—more mentally than physically. I've got to get some sleep."

I looked at him and spoke softly: "What is your real reason for suspecting Tim Burke?"

He said impatiently: "I've got four good ones, Connors. The only reason I give them to you is because you've been honest with me, helped me. You handed over the card and the radiogram."

He stopped. I said: "And the four good ones?"

Sonia faced us, standing near the port. A train whistle whined into the room, from the shore. Crozier looked at the carpet.

"Miss Vreedon knows three of them—or knows that *I* know three," he said slowly. "She might just as well know my fourth, too. The first one is the finding of the needle in Burke's mattress. The second is his swim to this yacht, and the fact that his explanation doesn't satisfy me. The third is that Burke is in love with Miss Vreedon, and that he has complained more than once about not having money prospects. He's even been bitter about it. Coach Mears knows that—and the crew doctor knows it. He wanted money."

Crozier paused. Sonia Vreedon was standing motionlessly, her eyes on his face.

"Burke didn't intend to kill Babe Harron," Crozier said. "Either there was a mistake in the dose—or the effect on Harron was more severe than on the usual person. Morphine is difficult to handle, when you use it in a large dose. This dose was large, though Doctor Bailey, of Vassar Hospital, stated that some men might have survived. He expressed doubt, however, and said that for the average, healthy man the dose would have killed in about thirty minutes. He thinks it required over forty to kill Harron, which means that the stroke might have received the injection in the boathouse or in the shell. And the time limit is uncertain, in any case. The point is that I believe Harron was to be drugged for a collapse—but not to be murdered. Therefore Burke's act did not seem so terrible to him."

Sonia said scornfully: "Not terrible—to betray eight other men in the shell—his coach, the college, thousands of others! Not terrible—to drug a friend?"

"Not terrible—compared to murder," the gray-haired one said quietly.

There was a little silence. I said:

"But *that's* not your fourth reason. I'm willing to agree the death was not intended."

Crozier shook his head. He took his eyes away from mine and looked at Sonia Vreedon.

"The fourth reason in that Vennell had known Tim Burke for more than four years," he said quietly. "He put him in college. It's true he was working his way through. But Vennell watched him. He did things for him. Little things, without attracting attention. And then, very suddenly, this last term, he stopped doing anything. There was no contact."

I looked at Sonia. Her face was very pale; she was swaying a little, one hand raised toward her breasts. I said mechanically:

"How'd you—learn that?"

Crozier smiled just a little, his eyes on mine.

"Vennell told me, before he was murdered!" he said in a hard voice. "He didn't want to tell me—but he spoke—"

We were both on our feet as Sonia Vreedon uttered a little cry. It was a strangled, low cry—and then she was slipping downward, toward the carpet. I caught her in my arms as her knees struck, and she was pitching forward. She was ghastly white. Lifting her, I carried her toward the divan at one end of the room. Crozier said very steadily:

"Why should a woman be so shocked—who has nothing to fear for the man she loves?"

·10·

TENDER BEHIND

It was almost three o'clock when I reached Suite B. Mick O'Rourke was lying on the bed, legs spread, and reading the comic section of what happened to be an old Sunday paper. He chuckled and let it drop to the floor as I closed the door behind me and stood looking at his big figure.

"It ain't so good as *Mickey Mouse*," he stated cheerfully. "Pa falls out of an airplane right down to his own house. And there's Ma—waitin' on the roof with a rolling pin."

I leaned against the door and nodded my head a little.

"That's a lot better than falling out of a yacht into the Tombs," I said.

Mick stopped grinning. He shook his head from side to side and made clicking sounds.

"I feel pretty sorry for Vennell, Al," he muttered. "And that stroke, Harron, too."

I said: "Do you?"

The big fellow sat up and swung his legs to the floor. He was wearing his trick pajamas, and the arrangement of color and design didn't make him look any smaller.

"Sure I do, Al," he said. "I been answering a lot of questions, but it don't seem to help much."

I shook my head. "That's too bad," I said.

Mick didn't like the sound of my voice. He frowned at me.

"What's eating you, Al?" he breathed.

I went over and sat in the chair beside my bed. Mick kept watching me with his big eyes.

"How did you answer the one about the reason you were aboard?" I asked.

Mick shrugged. "I gave it to 'em straight," he replied. "This ain't the time to kid."

I said: "It's nice to know you realize that, Mick."

He narrowed his eyes and leaned toward me a little. He spoke softly and slowly.

"You think I did in Vennell, Al?"

I shook my head and tried a laugh that was a little too strained to be worth much.

"It's this way, Mick," I told him, "*I* can think, but it doesn't mean so much. What's Risdon think?"

Mick grinned. "He thinks I finished Vennell," he stated grimly. "He hasn't exactly said so, but I've got a strong hunch he thinks it."

I nodded. "Why does he think it, Mick?" I asked.

The big fellow swore very softly. "I got a record he don't like, and maybe you've been talking to him, Al."

I said: "About what?"

Mick drew a deep breath, "About this and that," he said grimly.

I shook my head. "I haven't," I said. "But I figure that both Crozier and Risdon suspect you, big boy."

Mick shrugged. "Not many guys climb into the hot seat because they were just suspected," he muttered.

"A lot of them have got *started* in that direction because they were just suspected," I reminded.

The big fellow frowned at me. "What's the idea, Al—you figure I'm in a tough spot?"

I nodded. ''What were you doing when the main switch was jerked over?'' I asked. ''How about the shots?''

Mick nodded. ''I've answered that one a few times, too. It was hot and I didn't want to be inside the big room. I was wandering around, down below. I'd just picked up the funny sheet, down near the engine room, and I was looking for someone to tell me it was all right to take along.''

I said grimly: ''You're getting careful in your old age.''

Mick looked hurt. ''I didn't see anyone, so I came up on deck. I was folding up the paper to put it in my pocket, when I thought I saw a guy swimming away from the yacht. I was near the rail, on the starboard side. There was some light behind me, but it went out. Then it came on again. Then there was a shot. I figured someone had discovered the guy I'd seen swimming. I yelled at him—and when he kept on swimming, I fired one shot. but I saw right away it wasn't any use. The lights were out, and then I heard Vennell call my name. I was forward of his cabin, and I had to bet inside. It was black, but I kept moving, and I yelled that I was coming. You know the rest.''

I said: ''Did Crozier look at your gun?''

Mick said: ''Sure—and there was one bullet gone.''

I nodded. ''Naturally,'' I said.

Mick smiled peculiarly. ''Guns are like that,'' he said.

I said: ''You didn't say anything about the swimmer—in Vennell's cabin.''

Mick frowned. ''Maybe I was wrong,'' he said slowly. ''It might not have been a swimmer.''

I swore at him. ''Yet you took a shot at something—and you heard another shot, first.''

He nodded. ''Didn't you hear two shots, Al?'' he asked.

I looked at him for several seconds without speaking. Then I said:

"Neither Risdon nor Crozier can find anyone who fired that other shot. There's been a gun search—and they haven't found the gun."

The big fellow grunted. "The guy might have got worried, and tossed it overboard."

I said: "What would he be worried about?"

Mich shrugged his big shoulders. "It might have been one of the females," he said. "A little quick on the trigger—sort of nervous."

I smiled a little. "Like you were," I said.

Mick nodded, his eyes serious. "I'll have to cut down on the cigarettes," he muttered.

I lighted one and watched him for a little while. I was about to speak, but he got there first.

"You heard Vennell yell—and you heard me yell that I was coming, didn't you?" he asked.

I nodded. "It's a swell point," I agreed. "But don't work it up too much."

He just looked at me with his eyes expressionless. There was a short silence. He said:

"Where was this guy Risdon—he didn't get into Vennell's cabin until we'd been there a few minutes."

I smiled grimly. "Think maybe *he* did for Vennell?" I asked. "You heard what he said—he turned down the passageway and got out on the deck. He wanted to stop anyone from getting overboard."

Mick O'Rourke made another clicking sound with his tongue and the roof of his mouth.

"He's a quick thinker, eh?" he said.

I shrugged. "Someone murdered Eric Vennell," I stated. "And someone murdered Babe Harron. You didn't get to Harron, Mick, but Vennell might have made a mistake."

Mick closed his eyes. "What sort of a mistake?" he asked.

I said: "This fellow Crozier has been working pretty smoothly. He was with Vennell, just before the lights went out. He had Vennell talking. He says that Eric was only half conscious, but he was getting something out of his head that made sense. Perhaps he was—or maybe Crozier was using persuasion. In any case, Crozier told Sonia Vreedon and me something that hit her pretty hard. She fainted."

Mick whistled. "Yeah?" he breathed. "What's that got to do with Vennell making a mistake?"

I said: "It's got something to do with it. Crozier figures that you worked with Vennell—and that Vennell had Babe Harron morphined so that he'd be sure to clean up on his bets. He was shaky and he used the stuff himself. And Crozier thinks that maybe you thought Vennell might get talking. That would drag you in—"

Mick stood up in his bare feet and swore. He said: "Crozier's crazy as hell!"

I shrugged. Mick glared at me. Then he muttered: "And that made the Vreedon gal faint? Because she learned that Crozier figured I'd battered down Vennell?"

I said: "No—not that. Vennell put Tim Burke in California. He helped him some, the first three years. But this year he stopped. He got that far—Crozier did—when Sonia Vreedon keeled over. She's better now, but she isn't talking any. And neither is Crozier."

Mick narrowed his eyes and stood with his hands on his hips. He didn't look so dumb.

"And that was the mistake that Vennell made—talking to Crozier?"

I shook my head. "The mistake was that he didn't know how much *you* hated Dingo Bandelli," I said very quietly.

Mick O'Rourke's big body jerked. His elbows came up and his fingers clenched. The scar across his cheek twitched and seemed to stand our clear in the cabin lighting. He was breathing heavily.

"Go on, Al," he said in a tight, husky voice. "Spill the rest of it!"

I nodded. "I've got to," I said. "I'm bunking with you, Mick. I've got to have the truth. Crozier doesn't know this, nor Risdon. But I do. And you do. That wasn't a fake story that Vennell told—the one about his firm losing money for a big shot, who wanted it back. But he lied when he said he'd been put on the spot. He hadn't. The guy that lost that money tried to scare Vennell into giving it back. It didn't work. And the guy that lost that money just forgot about it. He went out to Chicago, got some other boys together—and cut in on a weaker racketeer's district. In a few more weeks he'll have all the coin back that he lost. That is, he will unless the police grab him."

Mick said slowly: "Grab him for what?"

I nodded. "For the murder of Vennell—the one who planned it, anyway."

Mick made a hissing sound and started to chuckle. I said:

"*That* was Vennell's mistake, Mick. He didn't know that you hated Dingo. And when he told us that story that wasn't all fake, *you* remembered that Dingo Bandelli was the boy who had lost the money. And you realized that Vennell had put out the story of being on the spot. And you knew that if Vennell were murdered—sooner or later they'd get after Bandelli. You hated him—so you—"

I checked myself. Mick's eyes were little slits. He was breathing evenly, deeply.

"So—*what*, Al?" he said very slowly and coldly.

I said: "After Vennell staggered away from the rail, you almost did it. But you didn't."

Mick O'Rourke smiled a little. His eyes widened and he showed his white teeth. He spread his fingers.

I said: "After Vennell staggered away from the rail, at the race finish, I followed him. There was a lot of storm. It was dark. I lost him. The chances are he didn't know what he was doing. It had been a terrific strain—

and he'd seen Harron collapse. I think you moved around the deck, Mick—and you were luckier. You ran into him."

The big fellow went over and sat down on the bed. He rolled over on his back, closed his eyes.

"What happened then?" I asked.

There was a twisted smile on Mick's face. He shook his head from side to side, opened his eyes, and sat up suddenly. Then he shook his head again. He touched his big toes on the floor, leaned toward me.

"Al," he said in a steady tone, "I ain't that kind of a guy. You oughta know that. Vennell slipped me five grand. I knew he was lying about something—I had the hunch right away that Dingo Bandelli was the guy who'd lost the coin on the Street. But I knew Dingo was back in Chicago, and I didn't figure he'd put Vennell on the spot."

I waited. Mick stopped smiling. "But I didn't go after Vennell, Al. Maybe I thought about it—yeah. Dingo was a louse—he tried to frame me more than once. He came after me with a knife—and he gave me this—"

The big fellow raised a hand and touched the scar on his face. He was scowling.

"But Vennell slipped me five grand, see? And I had a job to do. Maybe I was a little careless, at first. But after the race finish, I went after him, Al. After you, to make it right. I lost you both, in the rain and darkness. And then I cut across the deck—"

He checked himself. I said: "All right—don't stall, Mick."

He frowned at me. "Someone took a crack at me," he said slowly.

I stood up and narrowed my eyes on his.

"You mean Vennell hit you—and then you hit him?" I asked grimly.

He shook his head. "It wasn't Vennell," he said slowly.

He was telling the truth; I sensed that. He was frowning over it, and he didn't like to tell it—but it was straight.

"Who was it?" I asked.

Mick smiled faintly, with his lips pressed together. Then he got them apart.

"Torry Jones," he replied.

I stared at him. "Torry Jones!" I muttered.

Mick said: "Yeah. He'd been waiting for a chance to get square, you see? For me throwin' him over the side, making a fool of him. He followed me and took a crack. The wind helped him, and I went off balance, Al. When I got up and swung around, there were two figures near the rail. One of them was Torry—the other was Vennell. Vennell sort of slipped out of sight in the darkness—and when I started after Torry Jones, he was gone."

I stood stiffly, still staring at Mick. Then I said:

"You mean that Vennell walked into the wrong spot. Torry thought it was you—"

Mick said grimly: "It was black—and there was wind and rain. Jones made a mistake, that's all. But he knew it pretty quick."

I said: "Why didn't you say something—when we started the search?"

The big fellow shrugged. "I figured maybe Jones had done me a favor," he said very quietly. "As a matter of fact, Al—I didn't see Vennell go overboard. I just thought he *might* have gone."

I was silent for a few seconds. Then I muttered half to myself:

"Torry Jones, trying for you—and slamming Vennell overboard. That wouldn't be difficult, in the shape he was in. But he got back—"

Mick said: "We didn't find him for almost four hours. Where the devil was he?"

I said suddenly: "Torry Jones was the one who went

down the stern ladder and looked in the tender we had trailing out—the small launch. You remember, Mick? That boat was the only one over the side when the storm broke, and the captain had her pulled around back, let her drift. When the second office remembered that, Torry went down. He came back and reported Vennell wasn't aboard her.''

Mick said: ''Jees—that's right! And he might have been. He got a wallop—his head was cut. Maybe from the rail, Al. Nobody paid any attention to that little launch, after Jones came up from her. Vennell was groggy, but he finally got back to the yacht, flopped over—''

I said: ''Put some clothes on—we'll go along and see Torry Jones.''

Mick O'Rourke stood up and started to dress. I frowned at him.

''If you'd come through with this before, it might have helped—''

I stopped, remembering that Torry Jones had been in the saloon when Vennell had cried out, and when the lights had dimmed. Mick was remembering that, too. He shook his head.

''Torry Jones didn't do him in, Al—that was just a mistake. He was tryin' for me. When he got in a jam, he had to do some thinking. Vennell had been afraid of something, Jones knew that. And if Vennell yelled that Torry was the one—''

I frowned as Mick slipped into a shirt. I said softly:

''But Vennell got back aboard—and if Torry was worried enough, he had reason—''

There was a sharp rap on the door. Mick snapped the belt buckle of his trousers. I said:

''Who's that?''

Crozier's voice, pretty cool, said:

''It's Crozier.''

I opened the door, and the investigator came in. He looked at Mick, then at me.

"You're talking a little loudly," he said. "What's wrong?"

I looked at Mick, who was watching Crozier with narrowed eyes. Then I said:

"We're just getting ready to make a call on one Torry Jones."

Crozier said slowly: "Yes? Why?"

I told him. When I got through, he looked at Mick O'Rourke and said:

"Is your part of it straight, O'Rourke?"

Mick said grimly: "Straight as the road to hell!"

Crozier nodded. "Let's get started—we'll make it a threesome." he said.

2

Torry Jones had a small cabin at the end of a corridor. Crozier did the rapping on the door; he rapped twice before Torry called sleepily:

"What's—the matter?"

Mick muttered: "He's a healthy guy—he doesn't lose sleep no matter what happens."

Crozier called: "It's Crozier—let us inside, Jones."

Torry grumbled something, using the word, "sleep" a few times. We heard him moving round. Griggs came along the corridor and wanted to know if anything was wrong. Crozier said sharply:

"Not yet—aside from two murders and a few other things. We won't need you, Griggs."

Griggs went away. Torry Jones opened the door and blinked at us as we filed in. He was wearing a green silk bathrobe that wasn't so gaudy as Mick's, but that was bad enough. He shut the door behind us.

"I've got to sleep—even if some pretty nasty things have happened," he apologized.

Crozier nodded. Mick said: "You lost a lot of it when you flew the Atlantic."

Torry narrowed his eyes on the big fellow's. He said: "Now, listen—you big slob—"

Crozier raised his right hand a little.

"Cut the yelling," he said sharply. "When you went down the ladder over the stern, about fifteen minutes after Vennell disappeared, during the storm—"

I said: "Sorry, Crozier—but Jones went down to the launch after about thirty minutes."

Crozier nodded. "Thirty minutes after Vennell disappeared, then. You got down to the launch. What did you see in it?"

Torry Jones looked surprised. He smiled a little.

"The usual things a launch has," he said. "It was pretty wet, but partly covered with tarpaulin."

Crozier nodded almost pleasantly. "You had a flashlight?" he asked.

Torry nodded. Mick said: "You didn't see Vennell aboard the launch?"

The flier shook his head. He moved his tongue over an upper lip and fumbled around the room for cigarettes. I gave him one of mine and lighted it for him.

Crozier said: "It's a bad time to make mistakes, Jones. Everything counts. You sure Vennell hadn't dragged himself aboard the tender?"

Torry swore, "Of course," he muttered. "I got eyes haven't I?"

Mick said quietly: "You didn't use 'em too well when you figured Vennell was me—and knocked him overboard!"

Torry sucked in a sharp breath. He started a smile that was pretty shaky. I said:

"You volunteered pretty quick—to go down and look in the tender."

Torry muttered: "I don't know what you're gettin at."

Crozier spoke coldly. "No?" He reached out his right hand and caught Torry by the left shoulder. The flier swung around and slapped the investigator's hand away.

"Don't get hard with me!" he snapped.

Mick shoved me aside and stepped in close to Torry. I said:

"Careful, Mick—you're a big man!"

Crozier said: "No—take it easy, O'Rourke. We've got him. There was plenty of rain on that tender, Jones. But there was tarpaulin covering some of it, as you saw. That's why those on deck couldn't see Vennell's body. And you were in a hurry. The water was rough, and the little tender was jumping around a lot. Maybe you didn't notice that Vennell's head was cut. We found bloodstains, in the tender."

Mick sighed. He looked at Crozier with faint admiration in his eyes. I said:

"It looks like you didn't get Vennell *that* time, Jones—but you had better luck later—"

"That's a lie!" Torry Jones raised his voice. His eyes were staring into Crozier's.

The investigator from New York said: "Take it easy—don't yell. We're getting enough excitement aboard this yacht."

Torry Jones said grimly: "I hit him, yes. That was an accident. I was after O'Rourke, here, He made a damn fool of me. I hit O'Rourke, but not hard. There was a gust of wind and it swung me around. Something pitched into me, and I hit again—hard. Then I broke for it. I didn't know it was Vennell, or that he'd gone overboard. Then I saw O'Rourke—and Vennell was missing. I knew what had happened—I guessed what had happened. I was nearly crazy. When Rosecrans thought about the tender, I figured Vennell might be there. So I went down."

Torry Jones sat down heavily in a chair, shook his head. Mick said:

"Well—why did you leave him there?"

Torry said heavily: "I thought—he was dead."

Crozier shook his head slowly. I said: "Well—what of that?"

The flier looked at Crozier with wide eyes. Then he stared at Mick.

"I figured O'Rourke had seen me hit him. If you knew he was dead—O'Rourke would talk. But if it wasn't sure what had happened to him—"

Crozier nodded. Torry Jones said: "I couldn't figure why you didn't say something, anyway, O'Rourke. I was sure you'd seen me hit him."

Crozier looked at Mick. He said quietly:

"Why *didn't* you speak up. O'Rourke?"

I knew the answer to that one, but I couldn't see that it made much difference. If Mick wanted them to think that Vennell really had been put on the spot, and believed that sooner or later they'd get after Dingo Bandelli—

Mick said: "I didn't know just what to do, Crozier. It was an accident, in a way. And I hate to see a guy get the chair for an accident."

Torry Jones said in a flat voice: "He wasn't dead. He got back on the boat, after a few hours. He was probably in bad shape, and it took time. He had to get up the rope ladder. He might have lain on deck for an hour or so. And then he was taken to his suite. I was in the saloon, Crozier—when the lights went out. I swear I had nothing—"

Crozier nodded. He looked at me. "We've accounted for Vennell's disappearance," he said slowly. "He ran into Jones—and Jones was fighting mad."

Torry said thickly: "I'd been drinking—"

Mick grunted. "You still want to take a crack at me?" he demanded.

Crozier swore at the big fellow. Torry Jones said:

"I didn't murder Vennell—"

I lighted a cigarette and listened to Crozier say:

"All right—you get to sleep. It's a tough crowd to get anything out of."

He headed for the door. I followed. Mick said grimly:

"Pleasant dreams."

We went outside and along the corridor. Crozier led the way and didn't talk. When we got near Suite B, I said in a low voice:

"Why did Sonia Vreedon go out like that?"

Crozier's eyes held a distant expression. The three of us stood close together.

"She got a jolt when she realized I knew Vennell had been close to Tim Burke, out west. She says Burke was worried about Vennell. That was why he swam out. He wanted to find out if she knew how Vennell was betting."

Mick said: "Oh, yeah?"

There was a lot of doubt in his words. Crozier frowned at him.

"You'd better go to bed, O'Rourke," he advised. "You've been moving around a lot—and shooting at things."

Mick didn't speak. He looked at me, and I nodded. He went along toward Suite B. Crozier led the way into the smoke room, which was deserted. We took chairs that were close together.

"What do you know about Vennell, Connors?" he asked me.

I told him what I knew and what I'd heard. He nodded.

"Sonia Vreedon's story now is that Tim Burke hasn't too much background. No parents, only one relative, somewhere in the east. He met Vennell, and Vennell took a liking to him. This was before she met Burke. But even three years ago Vennell was anxious for Burke to go out for crew. And last year he asked a lot of questions about the Poughkeepsie Regatta—and Burke commenced to get worried. He got the idea that perhaps Vennell wasn't on the level, and thought he might be able to use him."

I whistled softly. "It's pretty well known that Vennell wasn't on the level," I agreed. "He was a sharp gambler, and he might have seen an opportunity here, even before the Street crash hit him."

Crozier nodded. "Burke and Sonia Vreedon stick to the story that Vennell was after him to take it pretty easy. A year ago—not that long ago, but at the beginning of this last college term, Burke and Vennell had it out. Vennell never came out in the open, of course. He couldn't afford to do that. But finally Tim Burke knew what he was getting at. They had a big scene, and that was the finish. And Sonia was afraid, because she knew Vennell. She tried not to show it, but she was worried. He must have known that she suspected him—but he went through with the bet on the short end, anyway. That shows he was sure."

I said: "And he was desperate. He needed money."

Crozier shrugged. "That's the girl's story—and Burke's. But if they had worked with Vennell—that *would* be their nicest story."

I shook my head. "They're not mixed up in this, Crozier," I said.

He smiled grimly: "They're mixed up in it, all right. What you mean is that they're not mixed up in the murders."

I said: "And Burke swam out because he had to know how Vennell was betting?"

Crosier said: "That's *his* story. But they wouldn't come through with any of it until I told them Vennell had talked to me."

"Had he?" I asked.

Crozier smiled coldly. "Not exactly," he replied. "He was wandering a little—and he kept saying that he was through—I'm through with you, Burke'—that sort of thing."

I said: "Then it looks as though Tim hadn't lied about the break?"

The investigator shook his head. "Why?" he asked. "Vennell might have been through with him because he didn't think he was going to do things right. But Burke could still have done them."

I shook my head. "He didn't," I insisted.

Crozier looked somewhere beyond me, and we sat in silence for quite a while. Then he said.

"Well it's like this—Risdon thinks O'Rourke and Tim Burke did these murders. He figures O'Rourke is strong enough to have finished Vennell. And Burke was close enough to use the morphine on Babe Harron. He thinks that O'Rourke hit Vennell with something heavy, after he yelled. He got rid of it—ran down the corridor and turned. Then he shouted that he was coming and headed back toward Vennell's suite. He thinks O'Rourke slipped Burke the morphine, and Burke stole the syringe from Doctor Vollmer the day of the race. Vennell knew about it, but he was weakening under the strain. So O'Rourke murdered him to stop him from talking."

I said: "I don't like the ideas—and I'm pretty sure Mick didn't kill."

Crozier looked thoughtful. "He's a strong man—and Vennell was hit hard."

I nodded. "Get the man who morphined Babe Harron, and you'll be getting somewhere."

Crozier said a little bitterly: "I don't think there's much more I can do. I'm not a mastermind, and this isn't one of those book stories where everything fits in nice, at just the right time. Any human being can lie—they can lie in groups. I think we've established the fact that Harron was murdered so that California would lose. We're pretty sure Vennell bet on Columbia. We've eliminated the reason for his disappearance and return. He was in bad shape, and it didn't require much reasoning to show whoever killed him that it would be a lot better if he couldn't talk."

I said: "What about the bets—they haven't been collected."

Crozier nodded. He tapped his gray mustache.

"Perhaps that was just another reason—for Vennell's

murder,'' he said. ''Perhaps somebody else thinks he can collect them.''

I said again: ''Get Babe Harron's killer—the one who used the hypodermic syringe. That's the important end.''

The gray-haired investigator smiled bitterly.

''With a killer aboard the yacht?'' he asked.

I said: ''*Is* Vennell's murderer aboard the yacht?''

Crozier nodded very slowly. ''*I* think so,'' he said. ''I've got men up above—and they'll be there all night. In the morning there'll be more. I can't say that we're getting anywhere, but I'm not through.''

He rose. I got up and stretched. He looked at me closely.

''Going to sleep in there with O'Rourke?'' he asked.

I nodded. He said: ''Got a gun?''

I smiled at him. ''You think it's that dangerous?'' I asked.

He had his eyes narrowed on mine. ''He might bother you some,'' he said in a hard tone.

I nodded as he went toward the door of the smoke room.

''He will,'' I agreed. ''When Mick snores, he bothers *anybody*.''

Crozier turned and looked at me with eyes that were hard and small. He shook his head.

''There's one person aboard—that O'Rourke won't bother,'' he said grimly.

I nodded. ''Vennell didn't have much chance.''

Crozier's feet made little padding sounds on the corridor floor.

''When you play the short end—you don't *deserve* much chance,'' he said softly.

• 11 •

SOMETHING IMPORTANT

When I reached deck, there were a flock of little launches circling around the *Virgin*, and the second officer was using a megaphone to warn them off. Risdon was talking loudly to the dignified man who had suggested the boat burned crude oil. As I came up near to him, he shook his head.

"We may be able to release those aboard the yacht today, and we may not, Mr. Condon," he said. "We're not playing a game, you know."

The dignified one sighed heavily. Risdon saw me and reached my side, at the rail. I looked at the boats puttering around.

"Reporters?" I asked.

Risdon said: "Yes, damn 'em. And photographers."

I nodded. "If there are any of either from the *News*, let them aboard, will you?"

He frowned at me. "I will not," he said. "We've got enough to do on this yacht, without answering fool questions."

I said gently: "Aren't you familiar with the power of the press? You might get a break—"

Risdon almost shut his greenish eyes. "To hell with the press," he breathed. "The only break I want is—"

He broke off. I said: "—to get the murderer of Babe Harron."

He looked at me sharply. "And of Eric Vennell," he muttered. "Or to make the murderer talk."

I shook my head. "You have to get him before you can make him talk," I said.

The detective smiled coldly. "*I* think we've got him," he replied.

I widened my eyes. "Something happened after I turned in, then."

Risdon said: "I don't know when you turned in. But I got very little sleep. We were at Tim Burke's most of the night."

I said: "That's tough."

Risdon shrugged. "I'll catch up on the sleep," he said.

I smiled a little. "I meant that it was tough on Burke," I said. "He doesn't know so much about this as you do."

Risdon didn't smile. "No?" he replied. "But maybe what he knows is more important."

"How about Mick O'Rourke?" I asked. "Have you still got him mixed up in the deal?"

Risdon said grimly: "You don't see anyone going ashore and taking the Central back to New York, do you?"

"I just came on deck," I replied. "I overslept."

Risdon nodded. "When we get through with this crowd, a lot of them will oversleep," he said.

I pulled over a deck chair and sat in it. I said in a casual tone:

"You're treating with two difficult problems, that's true. But you must bear in mind the fact that you are in contact with intelligent, sophisticated people."

Risdon looked as though he didn't believe that.

"Am I?" he replied. "Well, it doesn't seem to make things any easier."

There was the sound of heavy footfalls, and Mick loomed from behind a ventilator. He pulled up short as Risdon turned and faced him.

"I was up forward when the lights went out—and I ran across—"

Mick stopped. "Sorry," he said. "You didn't ask that question yet, did you? Not this morning?"

Risdon said grimly: "I didn't, but keep on repeating that answer anyway. You'll work it in at the wrong time, and then it'll be tough."

Mick shook his head. "Why?" he asked. "If I stand trial, I can say you beat the answer out of me."

Risdon muttered something that neither Mick or I caught, and went forward. Mick looked out over the little launches, drifting around.

"That fellow Risdon doesn't like me, Al," he said. "It hurts me here, too."

He hit his big chest two or three times, making a drum-like sound. I said:

"Don't be too funny with him, Mick—he's working pretty close to Crozier."

Mick blinked at me. "What of that?" he said in a surprised tone. "What have I got to worry about?"

I shook my head. "Nothing, I suppose," I replied. "But you've been answering an awful flock of questions."

Mick looked serious. "It's just because I'm big." he said. "Risdon and Crozier both figure a big, strong guy hit Vennell in the head with something heavy."

I nodded. Looking along the deck, I watched Doctor Vollmer approach us. The crew doctor was short and thickset. He had a rather heavy face and dark eyes. Mears came along behind him; the coach was tall and very sun-browned. He had broad shoulders and a very slim hip line. He was comparatively young, and there was a serious expression on his face.

He called: "Oh, Doc!"

Vollmer stopped and faced around. The two of them were within ten feet of us when the crew coach reached the doctor's side. Mears said:

"Crozier is looking for you, in the captain's quarters. Some more questions about where you kept the hypo stuff."

Vollmer nodded. He faced us for a second or two. He said to Mick:

"You're a big man, O'Rourke—not much trouble for you to see over people's shoulders."

Mick didn't say anything. There was a peculiar expression in Vollmer's eyes, as he turned away. I said:

"Another that doesn't think so much of you, Mr. O'Rourke."

Mick frowned. "What'd he say that for?" he asked.

Mears came up to us, shaking his head. "He didn't mean anything, O'Rourke," the coach said. "Doc's pretty upset about this. He's sticking up for Burke—and Crozier and Risdon seem to think Burke used—"

The coach shook his head again. I said:

"What do *you* think, coach?"

He almost growled at me. "They're a clean bunch of boys, my crew. Doc's right. Burke didn't do that. It's pretty terrible. No one did it—no person associated with the crew. That's my opinion."

I said: "Did Babe Harron see any other persons but those associated with crew, within an hour of the time he collapsed?"

Mears frowned. "Crozier has been working along those lines," he said. "There were several periods, short ones, when Harron was alone. That is, perhaps there were. But he was around the boathouse. Maybe in the shower room or looking over his oar. the boys get pretty nervous just before the big start. They find a lot of things to do. I was around the place—I saw Burke once or twice, asked him how he felt. He acted pretty well—a little nervous, maybe, but not more so than a few of the others. Babe Harron was around, too. He looked good and was pretty cool."

I said: "Did you see his back before the race?"

Coach Mears said: "Yes—but I wasn't very close to him. I saw his back from my launch, too—but again I wasn't very close. Tim Burke was in the best position to see any mark on the Babe's back. You know how it is—anything you haven't noticed before, on the back of the man you're facing in a shell—you notice it."

Mick said in his big voice: "And Burke didn't notice anything, coach?"

Mears spread his hands and looked out over the Hudson water.

"Up until this morning he said he didn't," he stated.

"But Crozier tells me that he's changed his story now. He says that he did see a small mark at the spot where we know the injection was made."

I stared at the coach. "He says that *now*?" I muttered. "Why didn't he tell Crozier that before?"

Mears shook his head slowly. "He says he was pretty worried about our finding the hypodermic needle in his cot mattress—and he figured he'd better not admit anything that would involve him. It wasn't much of a mark, he says. Something that looked a little like an insect sting, only it wasn't swollen."

Mick looked at me, "Burke's going to get himself into trouble if he isn't careful," he said.

Coach Mears narrowed eyes on the big fellow. He said slowly:

"Going to *get* himself into trouble. I'd say he's in pretty deep right now. And I can't believe it."

"Believe what?" I asked.

Mears shrugged. "You knew Vennell, you two. I didn't.

Miss Vreedon came to me this morning; she's pretty upset. She's in love with Burke, and he's crazy about her. She told me that the reason Burke swam out here was that he had heard Vennell was here, in the yacht."

I said: "We got up here pretty late—the night before the day of the race. Crew hits the hay early, doesn't it? How'd he hear it?"

The coach said: "Sonia wrote him, a couple of days before you came up."

I whistled softly. Mick swore. "The more those two try to explain, the deeper they get," he muttered.

Mears nodded. "Damned if they don't. But there wasn't much Burke held back from Sonia. Burke and the girl met the first year he was at California. Vennell was out there now and then. Tim thinks he was figuring on using him, even then. Vennell met Sonia through Tim. She liked him a little—she admits that. Now and then she joined a party on this yacht. Tim was along, if it wasn't during college term. And then Tim got the idea that Vennell expected him to do something. There were questions Vennell asked, things he hinted at. And he was pretty enthusiastic when Burke made crew. All this is what Sonia tells me. She feels, I believe, that Tim didn't do what Crozier and Risdon seem to think. And she was trying to explain why both she and Burke wouldn't explain the real reason for his swim out. They were both afraid that if it was learned Vennell and Burke had known each other—"

He shrugged. Mick said slowly, looking up at the tip of the stack:

"They're pretty sure Burke used the morphine."

Coach Mears nodded. "But they don't believe he intended to kill. They think that he made a mistake in the dose. They think Vennell made a guess at it—because he used the stuff. He got the morphine to Burke—they think that's why Tim swam out, either to get it or to get instructions. He was promised a large sum of money, with California out of the race. He wanted Miss Vreedon and needed the money. That's the police theory, if you consider Crozier and Risdon police.''

Mick muttered: ''They got plenty against the kid, at that.''

Mears nodded. ''They have, because they don't believe his story that he swam out to find out how Vennell was betting. He was worried, and Sonia says he was more worried when he was told that she thought Vennell was lying about having a bet on California. He was afraid of something.''

Crozier came along the deck, with Doc Vollmer at his side. They moved toward us, and Crozier said to Mick O'Rourke:

''Stand over there, alongside of Coach Mears, will you, O'Rourke?''

Mick said: ''Sure.''

He moved over and stood beside the coach. He was broader and a good six inches taller, in spite of the fact that Mears was a big man. Crozier tapped his mustache and frowned.

''That's all, Mr. O'Rourke,'' he said.

Mick came back near my desk chair and leaned against the rail. He said:

''What's that prove?''

Crozier disregarded the question. He addressed the coach.

''Babe Harron was just about your height, wasn't he, coach?''

Mears nodded. ''Perhaps a half-inch taller,'' he said.

I looked at Crozier, and when his eyes caught mine, I spoke seriously.

''I've a question I'd like to ask—if you aren't asking that things should be absolutely private. I'd like to have Coach Mears hear me ask it.''

Crozier smiled. ''Go ahead.''

I said: ''If Tim Burke's motive was to lose the race

for California—if that was the thing to be gained, why did he use the morphine on Harron? He was in the shell. Certainly he's read the story about the crew man who threw the race pretending he had collapsed. Why didn't Burke just flop over? He could have done it a little sooner, to make sure the others didn't pull his dead oar over the line."

Mears was nodding his head slowly. So was Doctor Vollmer—and so was Crozier.

Crozier smiled just a little. "That was one of the first things I thought of—in favor of Tim Burke," he said. "But it was one of the things that Risdon thought of, too. Others who have asked me that are Doctor Bryce, Doctor Vollmer here, Coach Mears, Sonia Vreedon, Miss Velda, Tim Burke—"

"That's enough," I cut in. "I wasn't claiming originality. I'll admit it seems obvious that Burke would collapse."

Crozier said: "Vennell was the one who planned to morphine the stroke. Not Burke. Burke did what he was told. Vennell was shrewd; we all thought of a very good reason why Tim Burke didn't have to use morphine on another crew man. But suppose Vennell thought of it, too. He would tell his idea to Tim, and Tim would tell me, if he were suspected. Well, Burke is suspected. And less than thirty minutes ago he asked me the same question that you just asked me, Connors. Why should he morphine a man—when he could simply collapse? That's the very reason he *should*—because the apparent foolishness of the act would be in his favor. And there is a secondary reason—if he collapsed there would be some disgrace. But the other way, there was none."

Vollmer said: "I wouldn't exactly say that." His voice held bitterness. "A crew member has been murdered—and all of us are more or less suspected."

Mick said slowly: "I didn't ask you that question—I didn't think of it."

Crozier said grimly: ''Well, it might have come to you later.''

Mick looked serious. ''I don't think it would have come later.''

Doctor Vollmer was looking at Mick with his dark eyes narrowed. He said:

''You're a strong man, O'Rourke.''

Mick took his big hands away from the deck rail and let them swing at his sides. He nodded, and slitted his eyes on Vollmer's.

''A little while ago you said I was big. What's the line, Doc?''

Vollmer said grimly: ''Eric Vennell wasn't exactly weak.''

Mick grunted. ''Oh, *that's* all it is,'' he muttered. ''You're trying to get across the fact that I swung something against the back of Vennell's head.''

Volmer's voice held protest. ''Of course I'm not, Mr. O'Rourke,'' he contradicted. ''I understand that you were his bodyguard.''

Mick nodded. ''Just now and then,'' he explained.

Coach Mears was looking at the big fellow. But he didn't speak. I said to Crozier, who was staring over the rail:

''How did you learn Vennell used morphine?''

''Doctor Bryce told me,'' he replied. ''He was his personal physician, and he didn't feel it was necessary to tell me while Vennell was alive.''

Mick said: ''Not even after he knew that Babe Harron had been morphined?''

Dr. Vollmer's eyes met mine. ''Sometimes Mr. O'Rourke is stupid, and other times he is very observant,'' he said with sarcasm.

I nodded agreement. ''Aren't we all?'' I asked.

Mick said with serious expression: ''It's my operation that causes that.''

Vollmer raised his eyebrows. ''What sort of operation?''

The big fellow shook his head. I watched Tim Burke and Sonia come along the deck. Burke was walking with his head down, and Sonia was talking to him, with her head close to his. Their arms were linked.

Mick said: "One doesn't talk about one's operation, Doc."

Crozier looked at me narrowly. Mick O'Rourke moved along the deck, toward Burke and Sonia. Coach Mears watched him go, then faced me.

"Unusual type, Connors," he said. "Changes his style of talk a lot."

I smiled. "When he talks highbrow, he's kidding," I said. "O'Rourke is just a big bum, quick on the trigger and not afraid of anything."

Crozier said: "And he's one of the persons we can't place, when Vennell was battered down in his suite."

I shrugged. Coach Mears spoke thoughtfully.

"Is it possible that Vennell could have fallen, struck the back of his head against something?" he asked.

Crozier said grimly: "Almost anything seems to be possible aboard the *Virgin*. But it would have to have been a pretty hard fall—and we didn't find blood on anything except the wicker chair against which his head rested. The chair could hardly have caused such a wound. And he cried out—for help."

I watched Mick stop near Burke and Sonia, saw the girl lean back from the rail and turn a pale face toward him. A plane droned overhead.

I said: "You haven't found who shoved over the main switch, or who fired the other shot?"

Crozier shook his head. "There's a switch box and fuses, out in the corridor wall less than twenty feet from Vennell's suite," he stated. "It's an emergency box—but there isn't anything mysterious about it. The main switch was thrown over there—it cut off the power in the generator. The one who murdered Vennell could easily have thrown that switch."

I said: "But we were going toward Vennell's suite, and Mick was coming the other way."

Crozier smiled grimly: "Was he?" he asked. "In any case, there's a narrow corridor running to the port-side deck from the entrance to Vennell's suite. Nobody was coming in that way."

Coach Mears said: "But we were outside there—Tim, Doc, and I. We weren't exactly opposite the door that leads to the deck, but we could see it."

"Not after the lights went out," Crozier muttered. "And you've said you couldn't see Tim Burke—after they went out. Or Vollmer, here."

The crew doctor said: "I started for the main saloon entrance, then stopped. It was very dark—the sudden contrast after the deck lights went out."

Crozier looked at the crew coach. "And you say Burke was right beside you—you could hear him breathing."

Mears nodded. "And I could hear that big fellow calling that he was coming. Then I headed in the general direction of the saloon entrance. When I got inside, there was a great deal of confusion."

Crozier said: "And you've stated several times that Tim Burke was right behind you."

The crew coach nodded. "I couldn't see him there, but he spoke to me as we neared the saloon door. He said: 'That was Vennell's voice.' That was all."

Doc Vollmer was shaking his head. "Whoever killed Vennell knew about that light switch," he said. "And that means it was some person familiar with the boat."

I nodded. Crozier nodded very slowly. The coach looked toward the boathouse.

"It seems to me," he said quietly, "that it looks as though we've got to get the one who morphined Babe Harron first. And I hate to think that man was one of the boys—"

He drew a deep breath, was silent. There were footfalls, light and swift, along the deck. The sound of the plane engine, overhead, almost drowned them. And then Sonia Vreedon was beside Crozier. She was excited; there was color in her cheeks.

"Mr. Crozier!" Her voice was excited, too. "I've just thought of something—something important! I want you to hear it—"

Crozier said a little harshly: "Something that will prove Tim Burke innocent?"

Sonia's eyes met mine. "I hope so!" she said simply. "It's important."

Crozier looked at me and smiled with his eyes slightly narrowed.

"Anything that will give Burke a break—that's very important," he agreed.

Doctor Vollmer said softly: "I feel sure that it wasn't Burke. Or any of the boys."

Sonia flashed the crew doctor a grateful glance. She looked squarely at Crozier.

"I'd like to tell you what I've thought about—and Mr. Risdon can listen, too, if you think he should. I'm sure it will help—sure!"

Her voice was steady and enthusiastic. Crozier nodded.

"We've gone over things pretty carefully," he said. "We haven't got anywhere in the Vennell murder, though I'd hold Mick O'Rourke on suspicion, I think. But in the case of Babe Harron—Tim Burke is—"

He stopped, shrugged. Mears said:

"There's strong circumstantial evidence against him, Miss Vreedon."

Sonia said in a voice not quite so steady:

"But you've got to listen to me—you've got to!"

Crozier shook his head. "I haven't *got* to," he said a little wearily. "You're prejudiced in Burke's favor. I haven't got to do anything. But I *will* listen to you"

Sonia Vreedon drew a short breath, smiled just a bit. She said:

"Now, please!"

Crozier nodded. The plane engine's roar was becoming a drone in the distance. The detective turned away, but Sonia stood still, her head tilted a little, her eyes on the plane. Then she turned away, too.

I looked at the plane, and when I looked away from it, Coach Mears was shaking his head, and Doc Vollmer was rubbing stubby fingers together and looking down at the deck surface.

"She's a fighter—that girl," Mears said in a low tone.

"It's simple enough—she's the daughter of a brilliant lawyer," Doc Vollmer stated.

I reached for a cigarette. "It's simpler than that," I muttered. "She's in love with Tim Burke."

• 12 •

SCREENED DEATH

Just before noon a big seaplane circled over the *Virgin* several times, glided for the water, and taxied near the yacht. It was a hot, clear day, and most of us were aft, under the awning. Tim Burke was nervous; he moved round a lot. And Risdon watched him closely. Burke had nice eyes and a swell pair of shoulders. His face and hands were burned almost black by the sun. I tried twice to get him talking, but didn't succeed. The only person he talked with was Sonia, and he looked at her more than he talked to her.

Carla Sard got to her feet and went to the starboard rail. Sonia had already reached it and was looking over the side. Most of us crowded around and watched the seaplane get beside the yacht. A tall, lean man called up:

"Mr. Crozier?"

Crozier was on the deck below. He said:

"Yes—we're expecting you. Get aboard, will you?"

The tall man got aboard. We stayed at the rail for fifteen minutes or so, but nothing happened. Tim Burke and Sonia were talking in low tones; she seemed pretty nervous. Rita Velda said:

"Crozier's probably sold the rights of the murder story to a tab, and they've sent the business manager up by plane with the contract."

Mick stared at her. "How could he?" he asked. "He don't *know* the end of the story."

Rita shrugged. "They can fake that," she replied. "Or maybe by the time they reach the last installment, he *will* know the end of it."

Carla Sard faced the writer and looked at her with contempt.

"What a mind you have!" she said. "You talk like that—with Eric Vennell dead. And the stroke—"

Torry Jones cut in. "Stop it, Carla—it's just her disposition."

Mick O'Rourke chuckled. We all looked at him. He leaned against the rail with his arms spread wide. They took up a lot of space.

"Just like it's *your* disposition to slug a guy down from behind," Mick said.

Torry Jones moved away from Carla Sard's side. His face was set grimly as he halted, several feet in front of Mick. He tried to keep his voice steady, but drinking hadn't helped his nerves much. And he was sore.

"Listen, killer," he said; "I'm not slugging you from behind *this* time."

Mick laughed at him. "That's right," he agreed. "You're just going to talk a good fight this time."

Rita Velda was smiling narrowly. Torry's voice quivered with rage.

"You—big liar!" he shouted. "You and Connors—both of you are lying. Vennell thought you were his friends, but you tricked him—"

I said: "Easy, Torry—you're just using a lot of words."

Mick took a hand away from the rail and made a simple gesture toward the flier. Torry didn't like it. He said in a voice that was pitched off its normal key:

"Where were you when the lights went out?"

Mick kept grinning. "Where was Washington when the lights went out?" he mocked. "Was he in the dark, you great big—"

Torry swore thickly, rushed toward Mick. Carla screamed, and Risdon's voice sounded from across the deck.

"Cut that out—you two!"

Mick smothered Torry's first blow with his left arm. The second one caught the big fellow in the chest, but it didn't do anything more than make sound. Then Torry's feet were off the deck surface. Carla screamed again. Risdon called:

"Stop that—"

Torry's body swung up and outward. A foot struck the rail; his hands clutched for Mick's head. I called:

"That plane's—below!"

Mick ducked his head, grunted as he swung Torry Jones' body away. Torry made a grab for the rail and failed to hang on. His body went over the side, turning.

Mick straightened and stared at Risdon, who was at his side. The big fellow said in a frightened voice:

"Jees-he almost threw *me* over!"

Risdon muttered words I didn't catch. Tim Burke and Sonia were close to the rail—all of us crowded it. Carla shrilled:

"He can't—swim!"

I swore at Mick. He was breathing heavily, but he muttered:

"Jees—I forgot—that!"

I looked down at Torry, saw a man standing on the hull of the seaplane lean down and reach out a hand. The flier was floundering around, but his body was close to the plane. The man on the hull gripped him by the light coat he was wearing. Carla kept crying out:

"You murderer! You did it before—"

The man on the seaplane was pulling Torry aboard her. I heard Crozier's voice and got my back to the rail. Crozier said:

"What happened?"

Mick shrugged. "I was attacked—by that fellow Jones," he said. "This is the second time. By God, Crozier—he's strong."

Risdon said: "But you're stronger."

Mick shook his head. "It's my temper," he stated seriously.

Crozier spoke in a hard voice. "Now, you cut it out, O'Rourke."

Mick looked hurt. I said to Crozier:

"He told the truth—Torry rushed him."

Crozier said: "That's all right—he didn't have to throw him overboard."

Mick smiled cheerfully. "It's a complex I have," he said. "Whenever I'm on a yacht, and a guy rushes me, I throw him overboard."

Crozier nodded, but didn't smile. Carla Sard said in a raging tone:

"I want him arrested! He murdered Vennell! You know that, Crozier. This proves how strong he is. He's sneering at us—"

Risdon spoke to her. "We can't arrest a man for murder because he throws another man overboard."

I watched Mick lean back against the starboard rail of the *Virgin* again. His face had become expressionless.

"I threw him overboard *before* anyone was murdered," he said simply. "And I pulled him out again."

Crozier looked at Risdon. "Keep those two apart," he said. "You've got enough men aboard the yacht to do it. I've got other things to do."

Cy Dana, standing near me, asked "What other things, Crozier?"

The investigator frowned at him. "You'll learn soon enough," he stated.

Torry Jones' voice came up from the plane below.

"If the plane had been—below—you'd have killed me—you—"

His nasty words died as Crozier leaned over the rail and called down sharply:

"Get back aboard here—and stay aboard. Stop acting like a kid—we've got more important things to do than to worry about your personal grudges."

I looked at Tim Burke. The Number Seven oar of the California varsity was staring at Mick O'Rourke. There was suspicion in his eyes, I could see it there. And I couldn't help thinking of Mick swinging bare fists against Dingo Bandelli's knife, trying to beat him down.

The scar stood out plainly as Mick looked at Burke. The big fellow's eyes were narrowed; he seemed to read the suspicion in the eyes of the one who was suspected of Babe Harron's death. He said:

"What's troublin' you, Burke?"

Sonia started to say something, but checked herself. Tim Burke stood facing Mick. He said in a toneless voice:

"I've got enough troubling me, haven't I?"

Mick shrugged his big shoulders. I went over to the rail and looked down at the seaplane. Torry Jones was using a ladder to get aboard the *Virgin*, water dripping from his clothes. Crozier's voice was even and hard.

"If there's any more trouble before tonight, I'll arrest those involved."

I said: "Why before tonight?"

I saw Sonia Vreedon exchange a glance with the investigator. But Crozier didn't answer my question. Carla looked at Mick with her eyes filled with hate.

"I think you did it," she said fiercely. "I think you did."

Mick said: "Did what?"

Before she could reply, Crozier cut in. He spoke in a low, toneless voice.

"Never mind, Miss Sard. We can't get anywhere by thinking things."

Mick nodded. "Better go down and find Mr. Jones some dry clothes," he suggested.

Carla stood stiffly, her eyes shooting hate at him.

"How would *I* know where to find his clothes?" she demanded. "Are you insinuating that I—"

Mick groaned. I said: "Go ahead, Carla—Mick didn't insinuate anything."

The big fellow grinned. "I don't even know what the word means," he muttered.

Cy Dana said: "Maybe Carla doesn't, either."

The picture gal swung her body and glared at Cy. Mick said grimly:

"Sure she does—didn't she insinuate that I did for Vennell?"

Crozier shook his head slowly, looking at Mick.

"Thought you didn't know what the word meant," he said sarcastically.

Carla looked at the investigator and made a gesture with her hands that was not ungraceful.

"You see how truthful he is!" she sneered.

Crozier looked around the group and nodded his head. He touched his gray mustache. Then he shook his head. There was a suggestion of a smile playing around his lips.

"The trouble is," he corrected, "that I can't quite see how truthful any of you are."

He did something that might have been the first part of a bow, turned, and moved away. Sonia and Tim Burke followed him. Mick looked at me and shook his head.

"Being a detective—even that kind of one—it's a tough job, Al," he said, "I feel sorry for him."

There was mockery in his words. I frowned at him, feeling uncertain. But Carla Sard didn't feel that way.

"Being a murderer is a tough job, too, Mr. O'Rourke," she said coldly. "I feel sorry for—"

She stopped as Mick lowered his head and took a step toward her. She drew in a sharp breath.

"—for any murderer," she finished in a hurried manner.

Mick stopped and leaned down. He picked nothing from the surface of the deck and made the gesture of throwing it overboard. Then he smiled at Carla.

"Yeah—so do I, kid," he agreed.

2

When I went into the main saloon at four o'clock, they were setting up the machine. I stood in the port-side entrance and watched them for awhile. It was a motion-picture projection outfit, and there was a lot of it. At the far end of the room there was a screen. I walked down and stood looking at the screen. After a few minutes I went around and looked behind it. There was a curved, large loudspeaker mounted just behind the silver square. Wires ran to one side of the saloon, and I traced them to the projection machine.

I lighted a cigarette, and while I was doing it, Risdon came over and stood close to me. His greenish eyes didn't look so green. They looked weary. He said:

"Like it?"

I shrugged. "It's all right if they use it to show comedies. But I don't like drama."

Risdon said in a hard voice: "The title of this one is *Regatta*. It's a crew picture."

I felt my nerves jerk a little, but I tried not to show it. Risdon said:

"Crozier wanted me to find you—he's with Sonia Vreedon, in her cabin."

I widened my eyes. "Is that nice?" I asked.

The Poughkeepsie detective made a weary motion. His voice was grim.

"You and O'Rourke can't seem to get interested in important things," he stated. "You're sidetracked with a lot of bum jokes."

I nodded. "Once a columnist, always a—"

Risdon interrupted. "I know—but I think Crozier's giving you a last chance. I wouldn't laugh it off."

"My God!" I said, "am *I* suspected now?"

"You might know more about O'Rourke—than you're telling," Risdon said. "Anyway, Crozier's waiting. He's sort of taken things out of my hands."

I smiled a little. "Do you mind much?" I asked.

"Not with *this* crowd to work on," he replied grimly.

I went out of the saloon and along to Sonia Vreedon's cabin. The door wasn't closed, but I knocked anyway. Sonia called firmly.

"Come in!"

I went inside. She was lying on a divan, and Crozier was seated in a wicker chair, smoking. He offered me a cigarette, which I didn't take because it was cork-tipped. I picked out a chair; Crozier got up and went back to close the door and lock it. I said to Sonia:

"You may feel worse, but you look better."

She nodded, "I feel as though there's a chance—for Tim," she said.

Crozier came back and sat down. He said in a very low voice:

"Miss Vreedon got an idea—when she saw that plane fly over the yacht, early this morning. The rest of us had muffed it. They shot pictures of the race, from the air. Two planes—and one was down pretty low. One of them quit before the finish, because of the storm. But the other stuck. The cameraman was Eddie Tippen—he used some sort of trick lens, and he got something. His plane came right up on California—Eddie figured that crew was going to win, so he concentrated on it.''

I sat up straight. Sonia said:

''I told Mr. Crozier my idea—and he got right in touch with New York. The name of Babe Harron's father, and the fact that the Babe was murdered—it helped. They have sent us up a projection machine and a screen—and two men to operate it. They've sent the film that was shot.''

I said: ''You've seen it?''

She shook her head. ''It takes a little while to set up the apparatus—it's sound, you see.''

Crozier looked at me with his eyes slightly shut. He nodded.

''What we want you to do is to see that Mick O'Rourke hasn't any gun with him when he comes into the saloon, just after dark.''

I whistled softly. ''You still think Mick did—''

Crozier sighed heavily. ''I've given up thinking,'' he stated. ''It all comes down to this—we've eliminated certain people. People we're pretty sure *didn't* morphine Harron or murder Vennell. We've established the motive for Harron's death, and we've got a good idea that Vennell was silenced because there was danger of his breaking under the strain. But we haven't got the killer. Tim Burke is in the worst spot. Your pal, Mick—he isn't sitting so well, either. I want him in the saloon, and without a gun.''

I nodded. ''I'll do what I can,'' I said.

There was a little silence. Then Crozier said quietly:

''Risdon will have his men inside, and we'll have the California crew and all those connected with it out here. And those aboard the yacht, of course. The place will be pretty crowded.''

''If the pictures showed anything important, the company that shot them would have spotted it,'' I said.

Sonia Vreedon didn't appear to hear me. Crozier smiled coldly.

"Would it?" he said. "Something that seems important to us might not seem at all important to a motion-picture company."

Sonia Vreedon nodded. I said:

"Well, I hope you've got something. I'll try to fix it so that Mick goes in without a gun. But you could make sure—"

The investigator leaned toward me. He spoke in a hard voice.

"You've helped me a lot, Connors. That's why I've been honest with you. If I didn't think there was something in this idea of Miss Vreedon's, I wouldn't go through with it. But I don't want to make much fuss about it—and search people on their way in.

I frowned at him. "They'll know you're not just putting on a picture show for them," I suggested.

He nodded. "They certainly will," he agreed. "I'm attending to that. But I don't want any *one* person getting set to stand a shock."

I sat up straight and widened my eyes on Sonia Vreedon's, I said:

"You're going to—"

She shook her head. "We're just going to show some pictures of the race," she said very grimly. "It happens there is a long close-up of Babe Harron. It happens that he was photographed just before—"

Her voice broke. I looked at Crozier and he said quietly:

"Your job is to see that the big fellow gets into the saloon without a gun."

I shrugged. "Mick didn't do—" I started, but Crozier interrupted me. His voice was tired.

"I know—O'Rourke is innocent, and Tim Burke is innocent. Everybody's innocent. But the facts are that

Babe Harron was morphined to death. And Vennell was murdered in his suite."

I watched Sonia's body shiver. She sat up and said very softly:

"I know it will happen—in the saloon, when we show the pictures I *feel* it!"

Crozier's eyes were on mine. He spoke in a toneless voice.

"There is a chance. Miss Vreedon is the daughter of a criminal lawyer. She has certain instincts. She may be right. We're almost beaten—I can't hold the crew at the boathouse forever, or the guests aboard the yacht. So we're trying the motion-picture show."

Sonia said: "Al Connors—do something for me, will you?"

I said: "I think I will, Sonia. I'd like to."

She nodded. "Don't talk to Mick O'Rourke—about what's going to happen. Please don't."

I said: "Mick doesn't believe Tim's guilty—and yet you think Mick is."

She shook her head. "I don't," she said, "And I swear that Tim Burke doesn't know what our plan is."

I looked Sonia in the eyes. "I swear I'll do nothing but try to fix it so that O'Rourke goes in without a gun," I said. "But *have* you a plan, Sonia—or are you just taking a desperate chance?"

Crozier said, before the girl could speak:

"Does it matter to you, Connors?"

I said: "No."

He nodded. "Just circulate around and act natural until we start the show," he advised. "The crew will be out at six-thirty."

I stood up and smiled at Sonia. "I hope it works," I said slowly. "They'll drag Tim Burke through the mud if it doesn't, and I suppose that means they'll drag you through it, too."

She raised her head, and her eyes were clear, defiant.

"Yes," she said firmly. "It'll mean—just that."

Crozier said softly: "Sonia and I will handle the seating for the show. See me before you go into the saloon."

I nodded. Sonia said: "Thanks, Al Connors—you've been pretty square."

I couldn't think of any answer, so I went outside. It was hot, and growing hotter. I moved round the deck and listened to people complain. Their nerves weren't so good as they had been two days ago. I leaned over the starboard rail and looked at the Hudson River water. I muttered:

"Picture show—"

And I realized that Sonia Vreedon knew that nerves were on edge. She was a shrewd girl, keen. And she was fighting for Tim Burke.

I looked around the deck for Mick, didn't see him. When I reached Suite B, he was lying on his bed, blowing smoke up at the ceiling. I said:

"You might have killed Torry Jones—doing a thing like that."

Mick smiled with his lips. "I might have," he admitted grimly. "But I ain't been getting the breaks lately, Al. So he just got wet."

3

It was growing dark—I stood underneath the awning with Mick and watched the crew men filing toward the saloon entrance on the port side. Carla Sard tugged at my arm, led me some distance from the big fellow.

"They've got—the murderer!" she whispered. "They took pictures—"

I said: "Who told you that?"

She shook her head. "I've heard it—several others know it. I'm afraid."

I said: "Be yourself—you didn't murder anyone, did you?"

She shivered. "I'm afraid—because Mick O'Rourke hates me," she said. "And I think—"

Her voice died. Risdon called sharply from a spot near the entrance.

"Come along, please—we want to get started."

Torry Jones called: "Carla—are you coming in with me?"

She moved away from me, her fingers twisting nervously. Cy Dana and Don Rayne passed; Cy dropped behind the ex-crew man.

"Lot of rumors around," he said in a low voice, "Does the talk mean anything?"

I shrugged. Cy said: "Well—with Crozier and Risdon losing a lot of sleep—they may have got something."

He followed Rayne toward the saloon entrance. Risdon looked at me, then at Mick O'Rourke. He said with sarcasm:

"Care to join us, you two?"

I said: "Come along, Mick."

The big fellow reached my side. "You've got me worried, Al—with all that talk about me having a gun on me." He grinned.

When we reached the entrance, the lights had been dulled. Mick said:

"It's hot—and I ain't crazy about movies. I'll stay near a door."

Crozier called, from a spot half-way down the room:

"This way, Mr. O'Rourke. I've got a seat for you."

Mick looked at me questioningly. I nodded. The big fellow swore.

"I'm being treated swell," he said. "Just like they treat a guy in the death house, before he sits on the hot spot."

He went forward and I saw him take a seat near an aisle formed by the arrangement of chairs. The saloon was crowded; crew members were at the rear. I recognized two of Risdon's men, from the Poughkeepsie police, one at each of the doors leading to the decks. There were men at the door that led to the corridor, and several in uniform were present. Carla and Torry Jones were seated beside each other, toward the front of the room.

Tim Burke and Sonia were across the aisle from Mick O'Rourke. Burke was sitting with his head held low and his arms folded. Sonia was whispering to him. The others were scattered about; Don Rayne was in the rear, near the crew members. Cy Dana was up front, but looking around as Crozier moved toward the spot where I stood. Rita Velda was at the far side, near a wall. She seemed very nervous and kept turning her head. There was only a faint murmur of conversation.

I saw Risdon across the room and at the rear. Doctor Vollmer and Coach Mears sat together, Vollmer on the aisle. They were a few rows forward of the crew members. There was a humming sound from the projection box, at the rear.

Crozier reached my side and said: "Most of the seats are taken—come along forward with me—we'll stand by the wall."

I nodded, and we went forward on the left side. We went quite a distance forward, and I was about to complain that I shouldn't be able to see the screen, when the investigator stopped. We got our backs against the wall, and Crozier stepped in front of me, reached my right side. We faced across the room, and, by moving our eyes, could see either those in the saloon or the screen.

Crozier said loudly: "I guess we're all here. Close the doors, please."

The doors were closed. It was dark outside—the *Virgin* had no motion at her anchorage. I saw Captain Latham and the second officer, Griggs, and the woman with the loud voice. The blonde was nervously moving her head around, but most of the others were watching Crozier expectantly. It was very quiet inside the saloon.

Crozier said in a toneless voice: "We have some pictures of the varsity race. I have just one request—please do not move from your seats—regardless of what happens.''

His voice had grown a little hard. There was a murmur of conversation as he finished speaking. He looked toward the projection box and said:

''Lights out, please!''

They didn't go out, but they got very dim. I saw that two of the center lights had been draped. The screen was fairly dark, but the faces of all those except the ones seated forward could be seen. I looked at Mick O'Rourke; he was slumped low in his chair. Tim Burke was sitting stiffly, erect. His head was turned toward the screen.

There was a buzz, a clicking sound. And then voices filled the room. It was the boathouse scene. The California crew were taking out their shell. They talked; voices called to them. The sound was clear in the saloon. There was a sudden silence as Babe Harron came into sight.

He was very good-looking, with tremendous shoulders and finely muscled arms. Someone not shown on the screen called clearly:

''Go get 'em, Babe!''

Harron turned and for a second faced the camera. He was smiling a little. He nodded his head. There were other voices. Tim Burke was in the background; the camera panned and I saw Tim look toward it. He was not smiling.

Crozier said: ''Burke looks—a little worried.'' His voice was a whisper; his head was close to mine.

I replied: ''Sonia told you he was worried about Vennell.''

Crozier nodded. There was a sudden staccato beat from the screen—from the loudspeaker behind it. The shot was from an airplane, and the beat was that of the engine exhaust. There were shots down on the Hudson, shots of the boats and the flags, the crowds on each side of the river. The *Virgin* looked nice from the air; the ship seemed to circle over her. There was a shot down on the observation train, and another of several crews rowing up the river for the start.

For five minutes we watched shots before the start of the race, some taken from planes, others from launches. And then a voice said:

"They're off!"

The next shot was a long one, showing the start. California appeared to get away badly—it was strange, seeing this part of the race for the first time. The engine exhaust of the plane filled the saloon with sound; there were long shots from the air. I looked away from the screen, saw that Coach Mears was sitting very stiffly, staring straight ahead. Doctor Vollmer was rubbing fingers across his face. My eyes went to Mick O'Rourke; he was still slumped low in the chair. Tim Burke and Sonia were tense, their eyes on the screen.

The camera was shooting down from the railroad bridge now; there was no sound of planes, but the shouts of those on the bridge. The shells had spread out; there was a short shot from one of the following launches. The straining bodies of the crew men photographed well in the fading light.

There was a break in the film. Then suddenly the camera was in the plane again, and the plane was diving. She was diving toward one shell, but for several seconds two shells were photographed. Crozier muttered:

"California—and Columbia! Almost at the finish!"

My eyes were on the screen as the plane dove lower and lower. The light was bad, very bad. But the plane was flying low. The Columbia shell was lost from sight—the California shell seemed to rise toward the camera. I could see Ed Dale's back, swaying forward, straightening, as he beat out the stroke.

There was another break. And then there was a close-up. It came so suddenly that it was startling. Above the engine beat of the plane I could hear the exclamations in the saloon. Someone cried out sharply:

"Babe—Harron!"

It was the stroke. He was pulling an oar, but he was having a terrible fight with himself. His head was thrown back, his eyes were staring. His teeth were clenched, bared by his parted lips. For what seemed like an eternity of seconds his head and the upper portion of his naked body filled the screen. and they were terrible seconds. The slide rig took him away from us, brought him back. He was swaying now, and the special lens seemed to have brought him within a few feet of the camera.

His movements were slower, more uncertain. Water struck against his face, but he did not appear to feel it. I knew that Ed Dale, the coxswain, had splashed it there. I drew in a deep breath, unclenched my fingers. There was a sudden break in the film.

And then the sound of the plane engine filled the saloon again. Babe Harron's face was before us—the same tortured expression, staring eyes. The same swaying body, with slowing movements. And I realized that we were seeing the same scene over again, with the plane diving very low and coming up from behind the shell.

There was a rising murmur of voices in the saloon. The slide rig carried Harron away, brought him close. There was another break—and again the beat of the ship engine. And once more the face, tortured and tilted back, of the California stroke.

I turned my head toward Crozier. He looked away from me, breathing fiercely:

"Look there!"

I stared toward the center aisle. Mick O'Rourke was sitting erect now—he was staring at the screen. But there was no fear in his eyes, no pain. I looked toward Tim Burke and Sonia. They were both tense; Sonia's hands were slightly raised, pressed against her throat. Tim Burke's eyes held an expression of pain; his mouth was twisted as he watched the stroke sway before him.

Something seemed to turn my eyes to the screen again.

The sound of the engine had changed; perhaps that was it. But there was still a close-up of Babe Harron. His head half filled the screen—the slide rig seemed to shove him forward into the camera. And as his strained eyes stared into it, his lips moved.

My body jerked as I caught the word they formed. His head swayed to one side—the slide rig took him away —brought him back. And again his lips formed that word.

And even as I turned my head, and the sound of the plane engine died, Sonia's voice reached me in a fierce cry.

"Vollmer!"

Beside me Crozier swore harshly. I stared toward the crew doctor. He was on his feet, in the aisle. His short body swung around, he screamed in a horrible voice:

"No—no! For God's sake—"

He was running now—a sort of staggering run toward the rear of the room. Crozier cried out above the sounds of confusion:

"Lights! Risdon—"

The lights flared up. Doctor Vollmer had stopped; he swung around now, started forward in the aisle. Sonia was on her feet. She cried again:

"It was—Vollmer!"

And then Mick O'Rourke's big body was blocking the crew doctor's path. Vollmer swung his arms crazily, and Mick reached out his big hands. Vollmer twisted clear; I remembered his powerful shoulders. Mick stepped in and brought up his right arm. There was a thudding sound, and I saw Vollmer's body collpase. Mick stood motionlessly, looking down. Crozier's voice sounded hoarsely.

"You people—keep still—"

And again the voice of Sonia Vreedon, this time with a note of victory in it:

"It *was*—Vollmer!"

4

The crew doctor was slumped in a wicker chair in Captain Latham's quarters. Sonia Vreedon sat on the divan, beside Tim Burke. She was pale, and her eyes did not go to the doctor's figure. Risdon and Crozier stood near a port, watching Vollmer closely. I sat in a chair near the door. Vollmer spoke in a low, thick voice.

"I had all my money—in Vennell's firm. He invested it for me—gambled it for me. He lost. This was six months ago. I went to him, and he laughed at me. I went to him several times, and one time he didn't laugh. He said there was a way I might get it back. He was in bad shape. He was going to put everything he had on Columbia, and California must lose. He was using morphine—Bryce knew that. He got it to me—enough for one dose. I was to use it on Harron, before the big race."

The crew doctor covered his face with his hands, moved his head from side to side. He was breathing heavily. Crozier said calmly:

"Go on, Vollmer."

The doctor took his hands away from his face. He stared straight ahead of him, and his words were slow, toneless.

"I didn't mean to kill Harron. That was the terrible thing. But I had to be sure—sure that his exertion wouldn't fight off the poison until the race was over. I used a strong dose. There wasn't much delay at the start, but there was more than I thought. It gave the poison more time to get into Harron's system. Morphine is difficult to handle—and the stroke—died."

He was silent for several seconds, then he said in the same, dead voice:

"It was a terrible thing. But I was desperate and I didn't mean to kill. The money I gave Vennell—it wasn't my own. I had to have it back. Vennell promised me fifty thousand dollars. He said there would be no suspicion, that no one would think he was betting on Columbia. But I learned, before I came to the yacht, that there *was* suspicion. There were rumors that Vennell had broken under the strain. And I nearly went insane."

Vollmer rocked from side to side, covered his face with trembling fingers. When he took them away, he said slowly:

"I came to the yacht with Mears and Tim Burke. I had put the hypodermic syringe in Burke's mattress, because I was sure he *wouldn't* be suspected. I wanted to confuse things. Burke was in love with Miss Vreedon, here—and I felt her position would protect him. When we reached the yacht, I heard again that Vennell would be able to talk very soon. I didn't know what had happened to him—didn't know then that Jones had made a mistake and had knocked him overboard. I wanted to get to him, but that seemed impossible. And then the light went low. I was along the deck, a short distance from Mears and Burke. I knew the *Virgin*—I've been on her, out in California. I knew where Vennell's quarters were. I was off the deck when the lights came up, just inside the narrow corridor. There was a shot—out on the water somewhere. Someone celebrating, I think. It wasn't on the boat. The lights went down again—started to come up, and I reached the switch box. I knew it was there. I got a handkerchief in my hand, opened the glass, and moved the switch."

He paused. Crozier said grimly: "So that engineer, Faley, was telling the truth. You people didn't know it—but he said something was wrong with the dynamo. The lights went down twice, but started to come on the second time. They were switched off from above. I held that back, because I wasn't sure who was lying and who wasn't."

The crew doctor said: "It was black in the corridor, but I heard you, Crozier, coming along. I got into a cabin near the switch box—the door was half opened. I'd heard a second shot, closer than the first. When you got near the saloon, I left the cabin and reached Vennell's suite. He was alone, stumbling around in the darkness. He'd got up."

Sonia was breathing quickly, her eyes on Vollmer's. The doctor said very hoarsely:

"I called his name—told them we were trapped. I was afraid and my voice showed it. The first thing I knew, his hands were on my throat. He was breathing terribly. I twisted loose, and he screamed for help. He called O'Rourke's name. I was desperate. In the darkness I struck at him. I thing he was half turned—and I hit him in the head—the back of it. It felt like that. He seemed to be falling and turning, though I couldn't be sure. Then his head struck something heavily—he groaned and was silent. I groped for him—O'Rourke's voice reached me, saying he was coming. I pulled Vennell up a little—and got out of the cabin. When I reached the deck, the lights were still off. I went quietly along, until I was behind Mears and Burke. They were near the saloon entrance. I'd only been gone a short time—"

Vollmer shook his head slowly. I said: "Then Vennell *did* hit his head against something—the front of that bureau—probably. But Vollmer pulled him up to a sitting position."

The doctor muttered: "I'm telling you the truth—I didn't murder him. It was the fall—"

Crozier said slowly: "It was that position of his that got me, with no blood on anything except the spot where his head rested. But if you pulled him up—"

Sonia said in a low voice: "He must have been crazy with fear—must have thought that Vollmer had come to kill him, to play safe."

Risdon nodded. "He went down heavily—and that furniture in his suite is solid stuff. It just caved his head in—that bureau."

Crozier looked at the crew doctor. Coach Mears was

watching him with narrowed eyes, shaking his head. Tim Burke stared at Vollmer.

"And Babe Harron—how did you morphine him without his knowing it?" he said grimly.

We were very quiet. Vollmer stared down at the floor of the captain's quarters.

"Harron was in the room that had been rigged up with showers," he said. "It's pretty dark in there. It was about twenty minutes before the start of the race, maybe a little less. I didn't know what Harron went into the room for. Perhaps he was just nervous and moving around. I followed him in, but he didn't see me coming. I had the needle in my left hand—and a file in my right. The sort of file the boys use on the oar handles to roughen them up so that they can get a grip when the water soaks into the wood."

I heard Coach Mears suck in a sharp breath. Tim Burke muttered something. Vollmer said:

"Harron's back was to mine. I struck upward with the—hypodermic needle. I used my left hand, so that the injection would not be too perfect. I'm a doctor—"

His voice broke; he shook his head. Then he said dully, thickly:

"When he twisted around. I showed him the file. It had a sharp point. I said I was sorry—I hadn't seen him in the gloom of the shower room. I was taking the file to the other side of the boathouse. It was just a prick. I kept the hypo needle concealed in my left hand. It's small enough. We went out into the light and I looked at Harron's shoulder. I told him I'd put iodine on it if he wanted, but it wasn't anything much. He grinned and told me to forget it."

Vollmer was silent again. Coach Mears muttered grimly:

"Made him think the hypo needle was a file end, eh?"

Vollmer closed his eyes and swayed a little. He said in a voice that was barely audible:

"I used a handkerchief on the syringe. When I got the

chance, I jammed it inside Tim Burke's mattress. I didn't think it would be found—but it was, I didn't think Burke would have to stand much—''

He checked himself, staring somewhere beyond me. He said:

''I thought Harron would collapse—and I'd bring him around all right. I could work off the effects of the morphine—he wouldn't know what had happened. There would be fifty thousand—I needed almost that much to pay back—''

His head dropped, and he raised hands to his face again. Crozier said very softly:

''You murdered twice—and I don't believe you intended to murder, Vollmer.''

The crew doctor said in a smothered voice:

''I swear to God I didn't!''

Risdon looked at me. ''I had a hunch that O'Rourke was in on it,'' he breathed. ''I sure had a hunch.''

Crozier said: ''Vennell was pretending he was on the spot, to get everybody worried about something else than the way he was betting—was *really* betting. And to cover up the times when his nerves got ragged, too. And when Torry Jones knocked him overboard, that made it look more complicated than it was. I think he could have talked when we got him into the cabin. But he didn't *want* to talk, and Bryce helped things along, until that doctor decided it was time to watch out for himself.''

I nodded slowly. ''And Vennell brought a mixed crowd aboard, two newspaper men—he didn't want anything to seem covered up. He wanted it to look natural—''

Vollmer groaned and took his hands away from his face. He said very thickly:

''That face—Harron's face—his lips calling my name! I couldn't stand—''

His head dropped again. I looked at Sonia Vreedon.

''That was a very nice idea—'' I started, but Sonia shuddered and turned her eyes away from mine.

Crozier said: "You take care of Doctor Vollmer, Risdon."

He went from the captain's quarters, and I followed him. On the deck he said quietly:

"I don't think Harron knew the doctor had morphined him, poisoned him. That wasn't why he used the name. He was going out, something was wrong. He knew that. Instinctively he used the name of the crew doctor. And the camera picked it up. It had a terrible effect on Vollmer, though. He isn't a murderer—not hard, that way. It smashed him."

I said: "Harron *might* have remembered the prick—he might have guessed that Vollmer had done something."

Crozier shook his head. "I don't think so," he said. "But it worked out right anyway. Miss Vreedon pulled Burke out of a bad spot. The plane gave her the idea—she felt that Harron's face, if it showed much, would shatter something in his murderer. She was convinced we'd have the murderer in the saloon. And we did."

We walked aft, and I watched Torry Jones slump in a chair and scowl at the big figure of Mick O'Rourke. Carla Sard went over to Torry and touched his forehead with her long fingers. The flier kept smiling at Mick. The big fellow looked at us.

"How much was he to get out of it?" he asked grimly.

"Fifty thousand," I replied.

Mick said: "Fifty grand!" he whistled a few notes off key. Then he shook his head. "Crime doesn't pay," he said in a peculiar voice.

Crozier glanced at me with his eyes slitted. He went over and stood by the stern rail. I motioned to Mick and we walked forward. I told him things, and when I finished doing it, I asked him something.

"I can still see you swinging fists against Bandelli's knife, Mick. You hate Dingo. And you knew that he was the big shot that had lost a lot of coin through Vennell's brokerage house. You knew the police would learn that pretty quick—even if you had to feed the information to them. You were sort of looking for a chance—''

I stopped. Mick was looking very stupid. He pointed along the deck, and I saw Tim Burke and Sonia moving very close together. Burke had his right arm around the girl; their heads touched.

Mick said huskily: ''Jees, Al—ain't romance swell!''

We halted near the port rail. I said quietly:

''You didn't fire any shot at anybody in the water. You weren't in the saloon when the lights—''

Mick said: ''In the good old summer time—''

I looked toward Tim Burke and Sonia. I spoke softly:

''Tim *did* swim out because he was worried about Vennell's betting. And he had broken with Vennell—refusing to do what Vennell wanted. Sonia was sure he'd try to come out. She waited for him. She knew what he'd be thinking.''

The big fellow said: ''And you *still* think I would have taken a chance with Vennell, if—''

There was a peculiar smile in his eyes; his scar twitched a little. I said:

''Mick—I think you're wonderful—''

I half sang it. He said cheerfully:

''But you *may*—be wrong.''

I nodded. I looked out toward the boathouses, then let my eyes go toward the bridges and the water running beneath them. After a little while I said:

''You fired that shot to pull people out on deck, Mick—you were going in after Vennell.''

Mick O'Rourke's eyes got large and filled with horror.

''Jees, Al!'' he breathed in a husky tone. ''You don't think I'd have done anything like *that?''*

I smiled at him. ''Yeah,'' I said. ''I kind of do.''

Mick sighed. I watched Tim Burke and Sonia vanish into the shadows, forward, and I sighed, too. I said:

"Those two have been through a lot—I hope they get a break and there's a moon tonight."

Mick looked at me and groaned. He shook his big head slowly.

"You got a swell idea of a break!" he muttered.